GUNNISON

MURDER AT THE
ROARING JUDY

J.C. FRANKLIN

WAYFINDER PRESS / RIDGWAY, COLORADO

Published by Wayfinder Press, Ridgway Colorado
Printed in Ridgway, Colorado, U.S.A.
Type - Stone Serif

*"This book is a work of fiction. The story and characters are
products of the author's imagination. Any resemblance to actual
persons, incidents, dialogues, or events is entirely coincidental."*
—J.C. Franklin

ISBN 0-943727-17-0

Acknowledgments

With special thanks to Eldon and John, to Jean Rodman and Etta Weaver for their encouragement, to all of the members of the southwest Writers Workshop and the Los Alamos Writers Group for teaching, critiquing, and sharing, and a special thanks to the people of Gunnison County who make their community delightful and beautiful.

1

Friday evening the Sheriff's jeep slid to a halt on the graveled clearing just beyond the Roaring Judy.

"Over here, Sheriff. Body's over here!" the deputy called out breathlessly as he hurried to meet his boss. "No doubt about it; it's Big Jim Clancy," he spoke as he directed the older man toward the scene.

"Gonna be dark soon," Sheriff Stone remarked noting the sky. "See to it that the boys get the whole area roped off pronto. I mean pronto! God willing, Powell, we'll sure get back out here at first light." He paused then added, "Remind me to speak with the ranger about closing off this entire area until further notice."

"Lotta people gonna be some unhappy to have the Roaring Judy closed down. Ever since they caught that 38-pound brown south of the hatchery pond, folks've been swarming out here every day."

"Deputy Powell, I think we have more important business at hand to worry about right now."

There was still enough daylight left in the fading summer day for Sheriff Stone and Tim Powell, his deputy, to see that the ranger and the doctor were already deep in conversation, while three members of the Gunnison County Rescue crew were standing by out of the way of the police photographer. Two other members of the Sheriff's office were combing the immediate area and making chalk marks on some of the rocks. The entire group unconsciously came to attention at the arrival of the Sheriff.

Frank Stone, Sheriff of Gunnison County, Colorado was a formidable man. Tall, well built, with strong handsome features, he was a man whose presence commanded respect. Dressed in the crisp dark blue uniform shirt of his office, he also wore jeans and brown cowboy boots tooled of the same leather as that of the big belt and holster that held his gun. Stone was well known throughout the state as a man who could and would track down the culprit though he had to move hell itself to do it. A born tracker, he had the blue-gray eyes of a wolf when it came to searching for clues. Though of late his arrests had mostly consisted of local DUIs and a few burglaries that any lawman could have traced in the snow. One thing about Stone, he had few enemies. His sense of humor and fair mindedness had held him in good stead throughout the community for five years. He was active in all aspects of Gunnison life, even playing softball on the Hummers team.

As he looked over the crime scene and listened to the reports and suggestions, he was struck with disgust for the criminal who would choose to do such evil in this God given beautiful place. He knew the blood from the gunshot would soon fade and wash away from the river rocks, but that spot would be forever tainted by the memory of the killing. He had even brought his own son out here to fish along these banks a few weeks before. It would never be quite the same.

The Rescue team put Clancy's body on a stretcher and left the area. They spoke only in whispers as they returned to the waiting ambulance. Somehow the Roaring Judy seemed more threatening and ominous than it ever had before as long dark shadows reached out toward the crew from the towering trees.

In Crested Butte, Kate Mason unlocked the back door of her shop and went inside. Careful to take off her mud-covered shoes on the throw rug, she padded across the room in her stocking feet and dropped into the chair at the desk of her tiny office. Inhaling deeply, Kate opened her purse and took out the small handgun she carried. Hands trembling, she laid the weapon on her desk.

She sat motionless for some time just staring at the gun. The silence of her closed shop helped to quiet her nerves, but she could not calm the savage beating of her heart. She deliberately forced herself to breathe steadily and deeply as though she were pacing herself in a race. For several minutes she waited, just staring at the gun trying to decide what to do with it. Kate looked hard at the instrument so capable of causing death.

She was soothed somewhat in her perplexity by the atmosphere of her shop, Hummers. She had purchased the small old building at the corner of Elk Avenue and First Street when she moved to Crested Butte during the winter six months ago. It had seemed like the ideal location for a small shop dealing with anything and everything anyone would ever need to know about hummingbirds. Her hobby had long been her interest in the flying, jewel-like birds, and Crested Butte was known for its unusual collection of the species every summer.

With a lot of hard work and what had seemed like an enormous amount of money, Kate Mason had been able to open her business during the Easter holiday. The shop, with its dazzling displays of collectibles—every sort of hummingbird motif, enchanted the local buyer as well as the numerous tourists that flooded the western town in the various seasons. Kate had been unprepared for the great reception of her shop, but she was grateful for the opportunity to recapture the investment she had in the place. Hummers, the city leaders had told her, was a perfect addition to the historic old town's main thoroughfare.

Leaving the gun on her desk, she walked from the small back room that served as her office and into the large open room that served as her shop. Passing the collections of handmade and glass-blown hummingbirds she walked to the window and looked southward down the busy Elk Avenue that served as the town's main street. She knew she needed a plan, and she needed a means of disposing of the gun. For one awful moment, she allowed herself to remember the way Big Jim had looked lying there on the rocks. She watched the lights of the Victorian lampposts as they came on one by one up and down the street; then she turned away and went back to her office to hide the gun.

⋌⁖⁖

Crested Butte, Colorado has been called the "Edge of Paradise" by Sandy Fails in her book by the same name; but for many residents, Crested Butte *was* paradise. Very few citizens in the small, historic town were aware of the murder of Big Jim Clancy, and most were content in the knowledge that there were never any violent crimes in C.B. and for that they were thankful. Although many in the community might be labeled by outsiders as eccentric or individualistic, Crested Butte prided itself on the accomplishments of the town. Almost every store in town sponsored a host of activities such as softball, marathons or races of some sort, and festivals of all kinds. Crested Butte's uniqueness did not stop at the false-fronts of the old mining town but carried through to the various personalities of the hearty souls who chose to dwell in one of the coldest, snowiest regions in the United States.

They also chose the quaint village for its spectacular scenery, Mt. Crested Butte looming above with 827 acres of skiing in winter and millions of wildflower blossoms in summer. Crested Butte had received the coveted award of "Wildflower Capital of Colorado" and prided itself on the pristine environment of its land and surrounding area. Biology and botany laboratories stretched their field labs from the base of Mt. Crested Butte to the meadows and forest lands near the ghost town of Gothic. Activities crowded the calendar of the busy community.

Sheriff Frank Stone was only too aware of the many events going on in Crested Butte. He liked to participate in the various sports offered, and he even played in the softball league, though he lived in Gunnison and had to drive the 35 miles twice a week to the games and practices. He enjoyed the change of pace and the country atmosphere; plus it gave him an opportunity as well as an excuse to get together socially with the Chief Marshal of Crested Butte. In his line of work, Sheriff Stone believed he could learn from every lawman's experience and expertise. He had great respect for the Chief Marshal and was eager to discuss the death of Big Jim Clancy with him. Clancy, after all, owned property and had holdings in Crested Butte. Stone picked up the telephone and dialed the Marshal's private number.

2

The Gunnison County Sheriff's Office and Police Department had only recently opened in its new location on Tomichi Avenue along Highway 50 just west of the Gunnison Cemetery. Many folks in the city and county had scoffed at the idea of building out toward the eastern edge of town until they actually say the new, high tech building. It was a credit to the city to have such a new and useful facility, but Sheriff Stone was often heard to remark that he missed the "good ole days" when he could just walk downtown and didn't need to get into his jeep for every trip.

But, times were changing in Gunnison. The City Fathers had decided a year ago to undertake some ambitious programs to stimulate the local economy. Instead of relying on ranching, the college, and a few sport fishermen for the main income, the city had decided to entice light industry and mainstream tourism into the area. They were even making plans with the city of Crested Butte to rerun an old railroad spur once used by the played-out mines in the region. The plan was developing so that a terminal at the Gunnison Municipal Airport would have the capacity to whisk passengers directly and scenically to Crested Butte. Naturally, the city had arranged for a City Terminal as well so that tourists could spend their days shopping in Gunnison if they preferred. Tourists could also enjoy the evening and nightlife of the city without the worrisome bother of the long drive back to the mountain. All in all, it was an upward trend for the entire county and the police and fire departments had been the first beneficiaries of the influx of new dollars into the economy.

Sheriff Stone could only marvel at the way things were changing in the once sleepy community. At least three companies spe-

5

cializing in cold weather wear and sportswear had moved to town. A candy factory had opened, and the downtown enjoyed a complete facelift thanks to the increased revenues. Lots of locals were being employed by the Clancy Project at the entrance to Kebler Pass. Stone had heard that the construction was to be the site for an all-season amusement park complete with elves and bakery. He wondered about his source of information on that one, recalling the student from Western Colorado State that had told him the story one day at lunch in the nearby McDonald's. One thing for certain, he did know that he would be spending time looking into the Clancy Project now that Big Jim was dead.

"Powell, is that the Clancy file?" Stone questioned the deputy that stood in the doorway.

"Yes, sir. Got it right here," the younger man answered as he approached the boss's desk.

"Go ahead and sit down. Looks like we're going to be going over this for a spell. This file is heftier than I remembered."

Stone opened the folder and began to comment aloud:

"Manslaughter while driving under the influence. Nearly forgot that incident. A couple of years ago, up at Vail, he ran a stop sign and killed a young couple. Judge up there was a friend of Judge Winfield. Seems he bought Clancy's story about hitting an icy patch and not being able to stop. Breath test was delayed; Clancy, when he was tested, claimed he only drank after the wreck to calm his nerves. Evidence got away from them, Powell. Let's see to it that doesn't happen to us. Looks like he only got a slap-on-the-wrist kind of fine.

"Here's a more recent complaint filed by a Dr. Jeff Harper out at the Gothic Labs. States he believes that Big Jim was the one who filled his backside with buckshot in May. I remember we brought Clancy in on that, but the scientist dropped the charges."

"Actually, Boss, I was here when that happened. 'Member? Harper said Clancy would 'Get his eventually for raping the land.' It did sound like a threat at the time, but I recall that Big Jim just laughed and said something to the effect that it would take more than a freckled face kid to quake him in his boots. Dr. Harper always seemed pretty nice to me until that incident."

"I guess we'll have to see what Harper has to say now. I do know that people with a cause can be pushed to the brink to commit a crime. I think they call it a matter of conviction."

"Right, Boss. We're looking for a conviction, aren't we?"

"A little gallows humor, Powell? We haven't even received the coroner's report yet. I don't see how it can come back short of murder though. Everything we saw out there this morning looked like a brief struggle and shooting at close range. No murder weapon yet. Doc Kellog should have something for us soon."

"Kellog's filling in for the M.E.?"

"Yep, he's authorized." Then he added, "I got a note here from the front desk that Clancy was in a minor altercation earlier in the afternoon at the Elk Horn Tavern. Seems he and Chris Rawlins got into it over Chris's sister, Lacey."

"Pardon me, Boss, but what would an old guy like Clancy be doing with a 'fox' like Lacey Rawlins?"

"What do you think?" he answered the younger man and winked at him. "Clancy wasn't that bad looking. Some women like older men; besides, it's a known fact he had mega bucks. He was a big guy and unattached. Might appeal to a 'fox.'"

"Well, I heard at the coffee shop that he was seeing that new lady, Kate Mason, up at Crested Butte. You know who I mean?"

"Sure, I do. She owns Hummers; sponsors my team. Only met her once or twice. Real nice lady, fine looking too. I can see why Clancy would be interested in her. Still, she'd easily be ten years younger than him. I figure she's in her early, maybe mid-forties."

"I still don't see the attraction. Guess I brought Clancy in one too many times under the influence. Watched him puke up more than I care to remember. Never could talk him into trying AA. Guess he thought he was just partying."

"His temper always brought him in eventually. Got to be at least six drunk and disorderlies in here," Stone remarked as he closed the folder. "No doubt about it, the man had enemies. You know, Powell, we're going to have to go talk to Big Jim's partner. Clancy not having any family is probably going to make Jasper Wilson a very rich man."

"What time do you want to go?" the deputy asked.

"Give me about an hour. I want to get a search warrant for Clancy's house here in town and that cabin he keeps near Three Rivers."

☙❧

7

Chris Rawlins adjusted his sunglasses. The mirror only showed him what he already knew to be the truth; his black eye was going to show no matter how he tried to hide it. He hoped the professor would not make any comments in class about the injury. Summer school and a full time job were enough stress without the reminder of his run in with Clancy after lunch the day before. He had only stopped by the tavern to give his sister the house key she had forgotten that morning when he saw Big Jim put his arm around the slender girl's waist. That had been all it had taken for Chris to fly into a rage and start a fight with the older man. Needless to say, Big Jim had tossed him out through the door, landing him on his cheek. He had been angry with Lacey too, but she had a way of convincing him that he was being over-protective and that she knew what she was doing. She always complained that he wouldn't let her take care of herself, and Chris knew that was true. Ever since their parents had died, he had assumed the responsibility for them both. Now that he was in college and working, he did not seem to have much time for his younger sister, but she, too, had a job and promised to continue her education eventually.

Chris gingerly touched his eye. He believed that he would never understand his sister. He wondered why any girl with her looks and potential would want to work in a smoke-filled bar and fight off the likes of Clancy. She had mentioned that Clancy was a great tipper, but that hardly gave him the right to make moves on a guy's sister.

Chris smiled slightly and shook his head. He knew he would not have to worry about Big Jim messing with his or anyone else's sister again. If what the news report had said was true, Clancy would not be bothering anyone again.

∽:∾

Sheriff Stone and Deputy Powell left headquarters and drove to Clancy's house in town. After a brief look around, they decided to go on out to Clancy's cabin and see what they could find.

As the two men rode beyond the city limits, they could not help but notice the beauty of the countryside. The highway was only two lanes, but it was wide enough to be an easy, pleasant drive in daylight. As they traveled north and east from Gunnison, they followed along the winding trail of the river-hugging road.

Driving onward, they passed through wide, open grasslands and meadows as well as through narrow passes that curved precariously close to the swift stream not more than a few feet below. Both men enjoyed the outing to the countryside in spite of the grim task that lay before them. Neither of them ever felt very comfortable about serving search warrants. It almost seemed as an invasion of privacy, but they realized that in the Clancy case, any information could help them. At least, they reminded themselves, no one other than a possible hired maid would be around the place to disturb them while they looked. The ten miles from town seemed to pass by quickly as they approached Almont and the confluence of the three rivers: the Taylor, the East, and the Gunnison.

They turned off the main road and drove another half-mile along the shoreline, down to Clancy's cabin. As they stopped in front of the well-built log structure, they could see that the front door was ajar. They drew their guns as they walked quietly down the path to the front of the house. Several feet in front of the porch, Deputy Powell changed direction and moved silently to circle around to the back.

The sound of the swift-moving water tumbling over the rocks in the river was the only sound either of the men could detect. The heady smell of pine warming in the sunlight filled the air and did not betray an intruder's presence. Neither officer moved for several minutes until at last the Sheriff called out a warning to whoever might be inside, then entered the building.

3

Guns drawn, Sheriff Stone and Deputy Powell searched the cabin for intruders. Finding no one, they began to search for information. It was going to be more work, they decided, as they surveyed the mess left behind by the break in. Everything was in disorder and disarray. Every cabinet door was open and every dresser drawer open or contents dumped. Whoever had been there had left a disaster behind. Even the refrigerator door was open with some of the food spilled about the kitchen.

"Dang. Didn't expect anything like this. Should have had someone posted out here last night," the Sheriff criticized himself.

"No one could have known, Sheriff. Could have been some prowler heard about his death on the news this morning and decided to come out for some freebies."

"Yeah, I suppose, but somehow it doesn't make me feel any better. It sure isn't going to make our job any easier," the older man lamented.

The men were startled by the sudden ringing of the telephone. Looking around quickly, Deputy Powell spotted the obnoxiously loud phone on the kitchen wall. Taking a handkerchief from his pocket, he lifted the receiver with the cloth.

"Hello. Sure, he's right here. Let me just give him the phone. Hang on."

Sheriff Stone took the call. It was a very one-sided conversation with the Sheriff merely nodding to himself and asking an occasional question. After a few minutes, he hung up the phone and told the deputy the coroner's findings.

"We've got a homicide, son. It was a handgun, a .22 caliber. He was shot at close range, maybe struggling over the weapon. Bullet

10

went in his belly and right up into his heart. Real quick-like. They recovered the bullet, but there's still no sign of the gun. Doc also said Clancy had had enough to drink to choke a horse. Guess that's why he couldn't fend off his attacker."

"Where are we going to start, Boss?"

"Well, Powell, I think we just got lucky. In all of this refrigerator mess, I noticed Clancy is just like me."

"How so?"

"Uses these little magnets to pin notes to himself," he remarked as he took a small piece of paper from the side of the refrigerator. The paper he removed was not much larger than one of the many magnets on the refrigerator's side.

"Let's see if we can read this scribble," he spoke thoughtfully. "Looks like 'Kate—Fri. 9' and 'Buck Mon.' The rest looks like grocery items."

"That shouldn't be too hard to follow up, Sheriff. Probably had a date with the Mason lady for last night. I know for a fact that the foreman out at his project is Buck Hayden."

"Well, I'm going to call the office and have a team come out here and go over the place with a fine-toothed comb. See if we can get his housekeeper in town to come also and help inventory his stuff. We can see for sure that there used to be a television and a VCR over there on that stand. Maybe we can find out if there are any other valuables missing. I have a gut feeling this wasn't just a robbery."

꒰꒱

At the Roaring Judy Trout Hatchery, the ranger in charge of the area finished compiling the list of known visitors to the grounds the day before. Some of the people he had known by sight and recognized; others he could only recall the vehicles they were driving. All in all it was not a very long list as it had rained all day Friday and many had stayed away because of the muddy conditions. A few die-hard fishermen swore that fishing was best during a rain, and he had recognized those fellows. He intended to get his list to Stone just as soon as he could.

In the meantime, his entire attention was given to the team dredging the south pond. They had received word that the shooting had indeed been a homicide and that the murder weapon was

11

missing. Because of the depth of the pond and its proximity to the body, it was necessary to search the muddy bottom and reedy shore in case the gun had been tossed there by the assailant. Chances were good that it would be found if it were there.

꒕ ꒕

At Crested Butte the city was in full swing celebrating, once again, another Wildflower Festival. The weather was perfect with blue sky interrupted only by the smallest of white, puffy clouds. The surrounding hillsides were deep green with the sign of a well-watered spring and summer. At an altitude of 9,300 feet, the thin air made the splendor of the multicolored flowers stand out even more, and the hordes of photographers that had descended upon the little town were quick to search out the most advantageous points from which to take their pictures.

The Wildflower Festival was not only for nature lovers, but it was also for fat-tire mountain bike enthusiasts. Bike tours, phototours, and nature hikes were all part of the well-established tradition in Crested Butte. Artisans from the surrounding area also came to show and to sell their wares. Booths were set up along both sides of Elk Avenue and the street was closed to motor traffic. The entire downtown became one large pedestrian zone.

Not wanting to be outdone by the freelance artists and visiting tradesmen, the local shop owners also participated in the festivities. Each store had a small booth or a table and display in front of his or her own business. There was everything available for sale along the sidewalk of the historic little town. Antiques and fancy lace sat side by side with punk t-shirts up and down the thoroughfare.

Kate Mason's Hummers was no exception. Kate had made a small display of glass blown hummingbirds hanging from a multi-tiered stand of drift wood. Each little jewel-like bird was suspended by the sheerest bit of nylon fishing line. Hovering there, the little flyers sparkled in the sunlight of the summer day.

As Kate sat behind her table waiting for the next customer her thoughts were finally turned away from the memory of her last glimpse of Big Jim. She forced herself to focus on the lovely, lifelike little birds that adorned her display. She studied them as if they were as real as the ones that swirled around her window feeders.

She smiled to recall the pleasure the dainty creatures gave her. She had learned a lot about hummingbirds since her arrival in Crested Butte. If she had not met Jeff Harper at the Nordic Club when she first arrived, she would never have embarked on such a business. She had always enjoyed seeing the birds when she visited Vail, but it was not until she had received the large insurance policy that she had even considered moving to Crested Butte and the quiet countryside. As a newcomer to the community, she appreciated the company and fellowship the young scientist offered. She realized that she was almost old enough to be his mother. In spite of that fact, they had formed a warm friendship, and had spent many long hours discussing the environment and the potential threats to the planet's very existence.

Kate knew that the bright young man sincerely believed in the work he was doing. She had not told him yet, but she was going to see Judge Winfield in Gunnison about setting up a trust fund for Jeff to continue his work. She had no living relatives to inherit her money, and she knew that Jeff would put it to good use. If she had had a son, Kate would have wanted him to be like Jeff. Just thinking those thoughts brought tears to her eyes as she recalled the tragic death of her only daughter.

Suddenly, she found herself remembering once again the death of Clancy. She knew some folks would have considered it "good riddance to bad rubbish," but in the past few weeks, she had been able to befriend the man and found him to be a pathetic, lonely individual. She had learned during one of his drinking, crying spells that as a child, his father had beaten him terribly. Because he was so large for his age, his father had expected much more of him in his youth than he was capable of doing. He had confided in her that he had been glad when his father was killed in a railroading accident, but he had never gotten over the guilt. Maybe that explained his drinking, she thought.

She was almost sorry he was dead. Almost...

⚓

Back in his office, Sheriff Stone picked up the ballistics report. Reading through the details, he was struck once again by the amazement he always felt at the precision of the Forensics Department.

They always presented him such a clear and logical approach to the solution of any crime. Their many laboratory techniques, as far as he knew, were flawless and up to date. He recalled that the last time he had visited the firearms unit it had looked like an arsenal or an armed camp. There had been guns of all types everywhere, on every surface of the room. There had been more guns than three Elmer's Sporting Goods stores combined in elk season.

He was also particularly interested in the report on the crime scene as well. Footprints of the area provided impressions showing that an unidentified man and unidentified female were also in the area at the approximate time of the murder. There was one good thing about fresh mud, Stone pondered. He was not certain that the news meant anything. The prints could have belonged to a couple fishing earlier in the day. He made a mental note to call the ranger at the Roaring Judy and see if he had been able to put together any kind of list.

He continued reading the report. A hair from an unknown person was found on the dead man's shirt. It had adhered to the blood on the shirt front. The lab said further testing would provide details shortly.

4

"I think we better pay a visit to Jasper Wilson," Sheriff Stone advised his deputy. The two police officers arrived at the Wilson's home on Ruby Avenue, just west of the college. Since the Sheriff had asked his secretary to phone ahead, both Mr. and Mrs. Wilson were awaiting them. They both appeared to be very nervous, Stone noticed. Yvonne Wilson's hand shook when she tried to light her cigarette, and Jasper seemed to be spending an inordinate amount of time fixing some loose cuticle material around his thumb. While they drank the cups of coffee that Yvonne offered, both Stone and Powell had an opportunity to observe the couple.

Jasper Wilson was the older of the two. He appeared to be a lean, leather-toughened, out-of-doors sort of man who had begun to go soft from too many hours behind a corporate desk. His wrinkled, dark skin was dull except for the shine of his nearly bald scalp. His skull had a hollowed, sunken look of a mind turned inward too long. Although he was only in his early fifties, Jasper Wilson had a haunted look that made him seem older than his years.

Yvonne, or Voni, as she was called by her friends, was a dark-haired, dark-eyed beauty with a good figure that was starting to spread. Overly made-up with too-bright lipstick, she gave the impression of someone who had dressed in a poorly lit room and had failed to note the garishness of her colors. A few years younger than Jasper, Voni was known around town as a real "party girl." She was known to go off for weeks at a time to Vegas on gambling junkets, but no one around town had ever heard of her winning anything big. Stone suspected that Voni's gambling debts were start-

15

ing to add up and take a toll on the old man.

Powell too had noticed that the coffee table held a stack of Colorado Lottery forms. He wondered how much Mrs. Wilson played the games of chance.

"Such a shame about Big Jim," she whined to the others. "He was always such fun to be around. Always out for a good time." She spoke wistfully to no one in particular.

"A LOT of fun," the older man replied scornfully. "We were just about to enter into the biggest, nastiest lawsuit this county has ever seen, thanks to him. Company's probably already ruined if the truth be known."

"Now, Jas, Honey, don't go speaking ill of the dead," she warned him as she looked at him.

"I'm afraid I don't understand, Mr. Wilson," Stone questioned.

"Just a minor disagreement, Sheriff," Voni interjected.

"Minor, hell fire!" her husband shouted. "His shenanigans are going to bring the company down. Darn fool never did get the proper environmental permits before he started construction out at the Kebler Pass Project. Lied to me. Stood right there and told me a bald-faced lie about everything being taken care of."

"Take it easy, Mr. Wilson," the young deputy said to the distraught man.

But Jasper continued, "Why, if that no account hadn't drowned out there on the river, I'd be tempted to kill him myself!"

The Sheriff and his man looked at each other. Sheriff Stone spoke up, "Mr. Wilson, I don't know how you got the idea that your partner drowned, but it's incorrect."

Voni spoke up, "You mean it was a heart attack? I just assumed when I heard the news that he died out by the Roaring Judy that he fell in the water on one of his regular Friday evening fishing outings. Oh, what a shame. Poor man lying out there all alone."

"As a matter of fact, Mrs. Wilson, it wasn't a heart attack either," the Sheriff informed her. "It was murder."

The Wilsons looked at each other with panic in their eyes, wondering if they had said too much.

The Sheriff and his deputy took their leave and headed for the jeep.

The younger man asked his superior, "Did you buy their story about them being at the V.F.W. bingo game last night?"

"Shouldn't be that hard to check" Stone reminded him. "Our

Mrs. Wilson has a thing for games of chance, so I wouldn't be too surprised to learn that she was there."

"What about him?"

"That we will have to see about. I really can't believe he hadn't heard that his partner had been shot."

"What are you saying, Boss?" Powell inquired. "You think he was trying to throw us off the trail some way? He as much as said he'd like to have killed Clancy."

"Wanting to murder and committing the murder are two entirely different subjects. Big Jim had certainly made a lot of people mighty unhappy."

The two men returned to their headquarters. Stone went in to telephone Judge Winfield for an appointment to discuss some matters about the case while Powell prepared to go back out again to speak to the person in charge of the V.F.W. bingo game.

◦∶◦

Chris Rawlins wanted to surprise his sister with the new VCR he had gotten the night before. He planned to have everything hooked up and ready to roll by the time she finished work. Even though the machine was used, it was practically new. He felt lucky to have the machine since his wages were so low and they always seemed to be strapped for money. He just hoped that their new entertainment would not increase their electric bill substantially. They were having trouble making ends meet as it was.

Chris continued working with the video equipment. His cheek and eye no longer hurt, and his attention was absorbed in the electronics of his latest acquisition. As he prepared to hook up the last lead wire to his television set, he noticed a small engraving on the back of the VCR. It said, "J.W. Clancy 514-72-2552."

◦∶◦

It was late Saturday afternoon before Sheriff Stone left his office and headed for home. He knew that he would not be able to accomplish anything more on the case until Monday. He was thankful for the rest and a day he would be able to spend with his family and at church. He considered taking his son fishing, then changed his mind about going to the river. Maybe they would all take a picnic and hike up on Mt. Crested Butte or play some tennis. In any event, he wanted to stay as far away from the Clancy investigation as he could.

Deputy Tim Powell was also very tired by the time he returned home Saturday evening. It had been a long day. From daybreak, he had been on the go. First there had been the chilly morning standing around in the nearly-dry mud at the murder scene, then the hours at the morgue waiting for the report that was never ready until five minutes or so after he returned to the office. He had gone with the Sheriff to Clancy's home and to the man's cabin, and he had called on witnesses. He wondered if Sheriff Stone had forgotten that they did not work on Saturdays; that was why they had the weekend duty roster.

He would not complain, however. Sheriff Stone never ordered a man in the department to pull duty that he himself would not pull. Powell admired Stone, and he hoped to learn as much as he could from the older officer. In the meantime, he planned to stick to Stone like glue until they got to the bottom of the Clancy murder. After church the next day, he planned to ride his Honda out to Gothic and see if he could get a handle on Jeff Harper, the biologist who had implied that he would get even with Big Jim.

Powell knew he was young enough to blend in with the fitness-biker crowd that frequented the hills around Gothic. He doubted that he would be recognized, particularly, if he were out of uniform. He considered the possibility that he might not learn anything. Yet, the idea that he might learn something significant stirred his enthusiasm.

He believed that Sheriff Stone would be pleased with his initiative, and for the moment, that was enough to make the tired deputy smile. It was the first time during the day that he could remember feeling happy about anything. All in all, the day had been what he often referred to as a "bummer." After hearing the reports on Big Jim Clancy, he was surprised that someone had not done him in before Friday. More depressing than the arrest record and personal life of Clancy, however, had been the sad bitterness he had seen at the Wilson home. He could remember back when Jasper Wilson was one of the finest ranchers around, a kind, generous man who was always helpful to the community. That had not been more than ten years ago. He wondered what had caused the terrible change, and then he remembered Mrs. Wilson.

5

Sunday morning dawned bright and beautiful. The sun danced over the peaks of aspen and pine; birds were singing loudly everywhere. It was a day when all things in nature seemed to be in harmony. The fishermen of the county had long since launched their boats for the early morning catch while others in rubber waders stood in the water, casting for the elusive rainbow trout. Mist melted away from the lowlands as the land warmed and the day began.

By lunchtime, the summer day was proving to be spectacular, and Tim Powell intended to take full advantage of the good weather and ride to Gothic. He had planned to travel there on his cycle, but when he went out to his garage to get his machine, he noticed that one of the tires was flat. He had time to change the flat, but decided against it. He simply was not in the mood; he would drive his car instead.

It was a terrific day for a drive. With the windows down and the air whirling through his car, Powell felt almost as though he were biking without the effort. He suddenly realized just how tired he was and promised himself he would not be out long so that he could get a good night's sleep. For the first time, he realized how much of a toll the Clancy case was taking on his body and his mind.

As he sped along the highway, he noted the farmlands, homes, and river bends. When he reached Almont, he pulled in and parked at the Resort. Leaving his car under the pines, he went into the restaurant and was seated at a window table by a young waitress. He ordered a cup of coffee and a piece of pie. While he waited, he studied the view from the window.

From his vantage point, he could see the end of the turn-off road that led to Clancy's cabin. Although the cabin itself was not in view, the end of the drive was. Through a grove of pines, he could just barely make out the edge of the first cabin on the road; a cabin he had already investigated and discovered to be unoccupied for some time as the owners lived in Kansas and rarely spent time in the area.

He looked around the restaurant. There were very few patrons at the moment. It was after the Sunday brunch and lunch rush time, so he practically had the place to himself. He decided to take a chance when the girl returned with his order.

"Excuse me, miss," Powell began speaking while removing his shield to show the girl his official badge.

"Oh, Tim Powell, I've heard of you. Here on business?" She smiled a smile that told him what his buddies often told him; women were attracted to his boyish, good looks.

"Yes, as a matter of fact," he replied and smiled as he leaned forward slightly to get a better look at the name tag she wore. "Linda Lou?"

"That's right."

"That's a pretty name," he stammered then continued. "I was wondering if you were on duty for the breakfast or lunch shift yesterday?"

"Sure was, Officer Powell. Why?"

"Well, any chance that during your duties you happened to notice anyone going down that frontage road over there? You've got a good view of it from here."

"Of course, I did. Saw you and Sheriff Stone go by in his jeep. Can't miss his jeep. Plus all of the commotion down there after you all left."

"You're pretty observant," he complimented her.

She shyly acknowledged his praise.

"I was really curious though, if maybe you had seen another car go down there before us. Maybe when you were first coming to work?"

"Yeah, come to think of it there was a truck. But it was leaving the road, not going down there, just as I got here."

Deputy Powell sat up a little straighter in his chair. He was eager to hear what she had to say and asked her to describe the vehicle.

"Sure. I don't know whose it was, but I got a pretty good look at it. It was a blue Bronco. Had a front license plate with one of those crazy little birds on it."

"Crazy bird?" he questioned.

"Yeah, you know the type in the cartoons that's always being chased by that coyote, but he never gets caught."

"Ah, yes, a roadrunner."

"That's it," she agreed happily.

"And you are certain it was a Bronco?"

"Absolutely. It was one just like my *ex*-boyfriend used to drive," she emphasized the "ex."

"Thank you very much, miss,.....Linda Lou," he added.

"You are very welcome, Officer Powell," she replied and gave him that special smile once again.

"I may need you to sign some papers later. If you could give me your full name and phone number, I'll be getting back to you real soon."

Tim Powell determined to change his plans. Instead of going on to Gothic, he decided to drive down the side road once again to Clancy's cabin. He wanted to have another look around.

Powell walked down to the log cabin and stood looking at the place for several minutes. It was an attractive structure with a broad front porch and a natural stone fireplace. The building itself was sealed, so he could not go inside. Nevertheless, he was content to study the grounds and perimeter. He was not certain just exactly what it was that he was looking for, so he allowed himself a leisurely stroll around the place.

There did not seem to be anything out of the ordinary near the cottage. There were plenty of tire tracks left by the investigation team, but basically the yard and surrounding area were pin neat. The wood pile was expertly stacked, and it was obvious to even the most casual observer that Clancy had taken good care of his property.

Powell thought more about Clancy. He had not known him well, but he did know a bit about his work history, his arrest record, and his personal life was starting to be revealed. The young officer thought about the wealth the dead man had accumulated, and for the first time it occurred to him that perhaps Big Jim had a stash of cash hidden at the cabin. It would not have surprised him at all. He considered the possibility that whoever had murdered Clancy might

21

have known about the money also and come directly from the river to the cabin.

Powell was studying such a possibility as he wandered a few more feet down to the water's edge. He sat down on one of the large rocks at the shore and watched the water. He enjoyed the feel of the hot sun on his back as he looked at the crystal clear stream bounce and tumble through the swift current. While he sat there, a raft load of tourists went by yelling and waving to him, but in a half a minute they were gone around the next river bend and out of sight.

The young policeman cherished the clean, unpolluted environment of his county. He was glad that the local citizens took such pride in maintaining their resources. If there was one thing he had loved to do as a rookie, it was issuing citations for littering. "Every litter bit hurts" had been his personal motto in those days, and he still felt strongly about protecting the planet. He was starting to regret the fact that he had not gone on to Gothic to speak to the biologist, Harper, when something by the rock where he was sitting caught his eye.

Wedged in between two smaller rocks lay something white and red. At first glance, the deputy thought it was a scrap of paper; but as he reached to retrieve it, he stopped. It was going to require one of the little plastic bags he always carried. He could see that it was a half-smoked cigarette with a smear of bright red lipstick.

⌣∶∾

Monday morning at the Sheriff's Office was hectic. There was the usual pile of reports and citations to be sorted out as well as the growing stack of folders pertaining to the Clancy case. Sheriff Stone looked at his in-basket in dismay. It would take him hours just to do the routine items first before he could get to the murder investigation. He knew that he needed a better system. He asked his secretary to let Deputy Powell know that he would like to see him at one o'clock. By that time, he hoped to have the routine matters under control.

He began his work on the pile of incidents. There were several old-news matters pending; he pushed those aside for another day's attention. He picked up each report from the current stack and began to methodically dispense each one to its proper department.

Nothing came through the Sheriff's Office that Sheriff Frank Stone did not read. He believed himself to be blessed with a near perfect memory and a reading speed that out-paced many of the college kids he knew.

A memory for details had served him well not only in his job as Sheriff, but even before that as an Air Force officer and security policeman. University had been a snap with his abilities even though his grades at school more correctly reflected his love of and participation in almost every type of sport. He had been a good all-around athlete, but he had never achieved "star" status in any particular event. He figured that was why he still played on a softball team at his age and managed to shoot dozens of baskets every night after work with his son. He liked action.

As he continued through the reports, he read of a vehicle stolen from one of the major campgrounds between the Gunnison city limits and Almont. The report was filed by a New Mexico resident who was night fishing Friday at the time the Bronco was taken.

"Dern thing is probably half way to California by now. Friday was definitely a bad day in the county."

The Sheriff exhaled loudly, pursing his lips in disgust. "Doesn't help the tourist industry a bit. Ripping off the visitor's truck is a real 'no-no.' We're gonna get that sucker," he vowed as he reviewed the All Points Bulletin that had been issued.

As the work load began to subside, Sheriff Stone finally felt he could turn his attention to the Clancy case. He decided that he and Powell would call on Chris Rawlins and see for themselves exactly what the fight had been about. He still needed to go up to Crested Butte and talk to Kate Mason. While he was up in the area, he planned to drop in on Jeff Harper as well.

The last item of business that he attended to concerned the note found at Clancy's cabin. He asked his secretary to put through a call to the Clancy Project at Kebler Pass and get Buck Hayden on the line.

Deputy Powell also was hard at work. He had managed to trace the blue Bronco with the roadrunner plate to a Friday report of a stolen vehicle registered to Juan Chavez of Red River, New Mexico. Mr. Chavez, his wife, and another couple had arrived in Gunnison the previous week. The two couples had driven separate trucks but were staying at the same campground, so the Chavez family was receiving transportation from their friends. Their annual fishing trip was turning out to be more than they had bargained for in their retirement, and Powell felt sympathy for their plight. At least he could report that he knew the whereabouts of the Bronco on early Saturday morning. He sent a memo on it to his boss.

༝ི༔

At Crested Butte, Kate Mason waited patiently for Dr. Jeff Harper to meet her for lunch. Since she kept her shop open on Sunday afternoons, she usually closed on Mondays and ran her errands. She liked to spend time out of the small shop whenever possible as she lived above it on the second floor. It was easy for her, she had discovered, to spend far too much time indoors and absentmindedly let the beautiful summer days pass by her. She wanted to enjoy every moment she had left.

Kate looked down at the menu of La Bosquet then back up at the trees and the tops of the quaint buildings. She loved dining al fresco and particularly liked the French-inspired food as served by the restaurant. She was certain she would order the leek soup but was undecided whether to order a salad or a sandwich with it. She did like the way they prepared the traditional BLT with Canadian bacon. Kate sipped a glass of mineral water while waiting for Harper.

In a few minutes, the young man came hurrying along the brick walkway and joined her under the shady, wide umbrella. After brief greetings and chit chat, they placed their orders with the waitress and settled down to await their meals.

Kate spoke softly to her companion. "I went into Gunnison early this morning. Had an appointment with Grant Winfield."

"That old buzzard. Kate, I thought you knew better," he scolded.

"Well, it wasn't by choice. He was just the only legal counsel I could get on short notice, and I really had to see somebody."

"I could have driven you if you'd only let me know."

"Oh, no, Jeff. I didn't need any help. Besides, I had to see my doctor and refill a prescription, pick up some things at Safeway. You know how it goes once you get to the big city," she joked.

"Did Winfield help you?" he asked.

"Oh, yes. He was a bit reluctant at first, but he finally drew up the papers I wanted. It was all quite simple really. In fact, I have a copy here that I'd like you to keep for me if you would," she spoke as she drew a large envelope from her purse.

"Sure, Kate. What is it?" the young man agreed.

"Actually, Jeff, it is my last will and testament," she spoke somberly watching the expression on the young man's face.

"Oh, Kate," he spoke sadly. "I hate to think you have been worrying about this. You know you are much too young and healthy to be concerned with this."

"No, that's not true. I found out not long ago that these matters can't be put off. One just never knows," she answered softly. "When my daughter and her husband were killed in that terrible accident, I thought that my very soul had gone out of me. I'd been a widow for so long, and then my only child was taken from me. Did I tell you she was only 22?"

"No, Kate. You never told me her age. I bet she was a beauty if she looked anything like you," he tried to comfort her.

"Well, the point I wanted to make was that the insurance company paid me quite handsomely for my daughter's policy. The company she worked for also carried a policy on her life, and it provided double coverage for accidental death. It was that money that provided me with the means to come here and start my business. I had a lot of plans when I came here."

"I'll be glad to safeguard this for you. Don't think another thing about it. I'll put it in my safe at work," he reassured her and reached out to squeeze her slender hand. "Does the will have the beneficiary's address so that I can notify them in the event..." his voice trailed off, and he wished he had not asked the question.

Kate Mason, however, seemed to brighten up instantly. She sounded almost jolly as she told him, "Why, Jeff, I thought I mentioned it. You are the beneficiary."

⌁⋮∾

The more Sheriff Stone thought about it, the more determined he was to have the young man, Chris Rawlins, brought in for questioning. The report of the fight on Friday afternoon seemed too good a lead not to follow. There was always the possibility that Chris had decided to get even with the big man later in the day. He could have followed him out to the Roaring Judy that evening. He might have taken a gun along just to even up the size difference.

Chris Rawlins' arrest sheet showed that he had a prior for fighting once before as a juvenile. The fight had occurred over four years ago in the high school parking lot. That was quite awhile ago, the Sheriff noted, and he wondered why the boy's record had not been sealed at the age of 19. Stone suspected that the youngster's parents just had not wanted to spend the money to hire a lawyer to do it. Some folks just did not think it necessary, and other folks in the county were too poor to do it.

In any event, Chris Rawlins was going to have to learn to control his temper if he planned to stay out of jail in Gunnison County. Stone would not tolerate fights nor brawls as long as he was in charge of public safety and protection. It had long been his experience that persons who would fight in public were not beyond doing a whole lot worse in private.

After a few minutes, the Rawlins kid arrived at Stone's office.

"Am I under arrest, Sheriff Stone?" the boy asked.

"No, nothing like that right now," his words sounded ominous. "Didn't the officer in charge who brought you down here tell you that you were wanted for questioning?"

"Yes, sir, he did, but I was putting two and two together on the ride over here. Guess you know about the fight I had with Mr. Clancy last Friday."

"That's right, son. I thought maybe you could tell us a little about that incident. Of course if you'd like to have an attorney present, we can hold off on your statement."

"No, that's OK. I've got nothing to hide," he replied and told Stone about Friday.

While the younger man was describing the scene in the tavern, the Sheriff received word that Rawlins' sister was at the front desk insisting that she had murdered Clancy and that her brother was innocent.

"Kid," Stone addressed Chris Rawlins. "Your sister is here. Claims she murdered Clancy and that you didn't do it."

"Of course, I didn't do it! Neither did she!" he shouted and jumped to his feet.

"She must think you did it if she's that willing to jump in and take the heat," Stone spoke with a hard edge in his voice.

"Sheriff, I swear to you that I did not kill Big Jim Clancy. Sure, I was plenty mad at him at first, but I went on back to the college then on to my night job at the Quik-Shop."

"Quik-Shop next to Wal-Mart?"

"Yes, sir. The manager can vouch for me," his voice nearly broke.

"Should be easy enough to check. I'm not ready to make any arrests yet, but I do take all confessions seriously. You better tell your sister to change her tune, or I will hold her for obstructing. Is that clear?" he sounded tougher than he intended.

"Yes, sir," the young man replied as Stone showed him out the door.

As the Sheriff was returning to his desk, his secretary handed him a memo. It stated that Buck Hayden had not reported to work at the Clancy Project that morning. In fact, Hayden had been fired on Friday by Big Jim Clancy.

6

Frank Stone was a patient man. He would not rush into a decision that would cost him man-hours if he could help it. In his Office, there was very little margin for error. Each case had to be treated with caution and consideration as the citizens' rights and safety were uppermost in the Sheriff's concern. He was also a God fearing man who held to the teachings of his childhood. He served justice, but he did not pass judgement.

His reputation made him one of the most popular figures in the community; however, the very fact that he was so well-known and easily recognizable, made it impossible for him to do any undercover work himself. He had been more than pleased when he learned that Deputy Powell had done some sleuthing of his own over the weekend. Although many of the oldtimers and local residents knew Powell, Stone reckoned that the tourists and transients would not be aware of the youthful Powell's profession. The ambitious young officer was quickly earning his boss's respect.

While Stone was still contemplating Tim Powell's promise as a lawman, the deputy arrived at his door.

"Good news, sir," Powell reported. "Got that info you wanted on Buck Hayden."

"Great! Sit down and let me see what you've got." The Sheriff watched the younger man refer to the legal pad he carried.

"For starters, I could not get hold of the Crested Butte Marshal. He's out on a rescue case, some tourist up on the mountain slipped and fell, so they are bringing in the Air Life helicopter. Marshal's coordinating the show."

"Sounds about right. Wasn't too long ago he helped me with that chopper when I rolled my jeep last winter helping those stranded hunters," he reminded the young officer before he continued. "So, what did you come up with?"

"Actually, I think I got lucky. When I phoned the project, Jasper Wilson took my call. He's in charge now that Clancy is...gone. He really filled my ear about Hayden. Seems Buck has been the foreman out there since March, but he has been almost more trouble than he was worth."

"According to Wilson," Stone reminded him.

"I had heard something about it myself, Sheriff. Local gossip, but Wilson gave me some of the particulars. First off, seems that Hayden was chronically late to work with one excuse or another. Mostly he would blame his tardiness on that no account that shared the trailer with him. You know who I mean?"

"Yeah, I do, Ben Peek. We've had to run him in a couple of times. Can't forget that name," Stone replied and pursed his lips as though they had just tasted something sour.

"That's right. Not only did those two act alike, they even looked a lot alike. Anyway, apparently on Friday Buck told Clancy he was late because he had gotten in a fight with Peek and that Peek had packed up and run off in their old VW van. Guess Clancy did not buy the story, called him a liar and a 'no good user.' I presume that was in reference to Hayden's minor drug bust last month?"

"We can check Wilson's account with the other men at the site. A fight with the owner usually gets everyone's attention," the Sheriff noted. "How did they end it?"

"Clancy told him to vamoose and that he could pick up his pay at the downtown office. I checked on that too, Boss."

Stone smiled slightly at the young man's thoroughness.

"Buck Hayden got his check about four that afternoon. Put up a fuss in the office. Told the lady that issues the checks that he had been shorted a half day's pay. She says she told him to come back on Monday and see Clancy in his office; she did not have the authority to change the check."

"Have you pulled Hayden's file?"

"Yes, sir. Nothing major, but he was carrying a knife once when we cuffed him on suspicion of stealing tires."

"Knife, huh? No firearms?"

"No, sir. Wilson did hint around that he thought Hayden had stolen some of the copper tubing that they are using at the site. He asked if we could look into it, but I told him to contact the Chief

Marshal. That's his jurisdiction."

"Good work, Powell. We may have a lead now on that theft at the cabin. We've got an angry man and a stolen vehicle."

"Still got an APB out on the VW van also. Something should turn up soon," Powell spoke confidently.

After the junior officer left, Sheriff Stone turned his attention back to the memo he had received earlier. It was taped to an envelope. As he opened the envelope he was pleased to see that it was the list he had requested from the ranger at the Roaring Judy State Hatchery. As he scanned the brief list of persons and vehicles, he was surprised by two entries: the name of Kate Mason in the name column, and in the auto list, a Blazer tentatively identified as being one that belonged to Jasper Wilson.

∾∶∾

Kate Mason returned to her place at the end of Elk Avenue. She realized that she was starting to feel more and more tired each day. The doctor had warned her that the tiredness would increase, but she had not believed that the symptoms would manifest themselves so soon. Kate felt that she needed more time. There were still a few matters she knew she should clear up with the police. She just did not want to do it quite yet. The weary woman climbed the stairs to her dwelling and helped herself to the pills by the bathroom sink.

∾∶∾

Sheriff Stone and Deputy Powell had just left for the opening ceremonies at the Dos Rios Golf Club when the Forensic Lab telephoned. Since Stone was committed to helping with the ribbon-cutting ceremonies for the Community Athletic League Tournament, he was not available to take the call. The Lab assured Stone's secretary that they would contact him first thing in the morning. They were not only forwarding a copy of the report to him, but also, wanted to discuss the matter as well.

7

The Forensics Lab telephoned Sheriff Stone early Tuesday morning. Deputy Powell was also in Stone's office when the call came through. While the Sheriff was still talking, his secretary handed him the copy from the Lab.

"Tell the director that I appreciate what you guys are doing," Stone concluded. "Let me know the minute you get a final on the hair sample when it comes in. Take care, hear?"

The Sheriff glanced at the report to confirm that it described the details as accurately as the man at the Lab had indicated. Everything from the crime scene had been analyzed and categorized as much as was humanly possible. Stone shared the major findings with the young deputy.

"We've got two ways to go, Powell. The footprints in the mud at the scene that do not belong to our men nor to Clancy have been singled out as a lady's shoe print and a man's boot print."

"That's great, Boss. Got some sizes on those?"

"Right here. The lady is a size 6. Print is not too deep either. A lightweight, I'd say."

As he turned the page to a clean sheet on his legal pad, Powell asked, "What about the boot?"

"This and that. It's a size 10. Heel isn't too high. They think it's a Roper. Very common," the Sheriff added quietly. "Either of these could have been made by fishermen or campers earlier in the day. The lady's shoe is a bit on the dainty side though for anyone traipsing around out there unless she didn't know any better. Tourists do get carried away sometimes, park and wander off to have a look."

31

"You said two things, Boss. Did they get anything on that hair from the shirt?"

"That's the good news. They can spray all the plastic or shellac on mud impressions that they want; and they can make plaster of Paris thick as they want, but it still doesn't turn up anything personal. The hair, on the other hand, can be like a fingerprint, Powell. I'm sure I don't have to remind you of that. Besides telling us what we already suspected, that it was human, we've got quite a bit to go on."

"Female, right?" Powell asked. "He was hugging up Lacey Rawlins not long before that."

"Well, don't go jumping to any conclusions until you've heard the rest. Says here the short hair is from a female, Caucasian. The hair fell, was not torn nor cut from the individual. The natural color of the hair is very light brown but has been touched up with a bleaching product. It was a hair from the crown of the head, not the temple nor the neck. Lab folks say the coloring job was probably what the ladies call a frosting. They can not tell us the age of the donor nor how long ago the hair was grown."

"Sheriff, I'm amazed at how much they did get. I heard that they could tell a person's race by the hair. Something about the shape of the hair shaft and the way that the pigment was distributed," he suggested.

"That's right. They explained it to me in a seminar over there once. The Caucasian's hair has an even sort of pigment distribution, and the hair shaft is round to oval."

"Guess I better go find out more about this frosted hair though, unless you know something I don't know, Boss?" The younger man raised his eyebrows and looked to his mentor.

"You've got me there. My secretary might be able to get us some magazine pictures. Otherwise, I guess we'll have to pay a visit to the beauty parlor. How's that gonna look, Powell?"

Chris Rawlins had not been sleeping well. The journey to the Sheriff's Office had upset him very much. He was appalled to think that the officers were even considering him as a possible suspect in the Clancy murder. It bothered him even more that his own sister had suspected his guilt when she gave her confession. He had to admit, there were grounds for building a case against him. He did have that terrible row in the tavern that afternoon. Chris realized, however, that he was facing a very serious situation. The VCR sat right there in the middle of his living room with the name of Jim Clancy written as clear as could be. Rawlins knew he had been a fool over that VCR, but it had all seemed so harmless at the time. He felt certain that if Sheriff Stone were to enter his apartment with a search warrant, he would be as good as convicted. He tapped his chin hard with his own fist.

He had to decide what to do about the video equipment before it was too late. He wondered if Stone would believe him if he told him the truth. The only thing he knew for certain was that time was running out, and it was only a short while before the Sheriff or his deputy would be knocking on his door. He had to make a decision.

⌄:~

Deputy Powell asked the Sheriff, "Are we going to drive out to Crested Butte or take the rail?"

"Got to take the jeep. I know you look for any excuse to ride that Iron Horse, don't you?"

"Yes, sir. Sometimes I do. I also enjoy the drive though."

"Tell you what. You can take the rail back if you want. I've got a ball game out there tonight and have to take a change of clothes. We can drive separately or together. Your choice."

"I'll stick with you. Wouldn't want to miss a game."

"Take a change and suit up with us. You could use the exercise. Clears the head."

"Thanks, but no thanks, Boss. I'll be happy to be a spectator; though I will take some civies along and change. Never know what I might hear in the crowd."

"OK, Powell. You don't have to carry the detecting too far. You can take breaks. Trust me." The older man grinned at the determined youth.

The two men left the building and went by the Sheriff's house to pick up his Hummers uniform shirt and his ball glove. As they rode along the highway, they wondered what new information they would get from Dr. Jeff Harper when they met him at the Gothic Biological Research Station.

Gothic was only six miles north of Mt. Crested Butte. The road between the ski resort and the old town deteriorated to hard packed gravel maintained by the county as a seasonal road. Sometimes closed in winter, the road was only guaranteed passable by reliable snowmobile. Rutted and curving, the trailway wound its way along a high, shoulderless cliff, through dense forest, and passed open meadows that sported an exotic array of multicolored wildflowers. The isolation of the town helped it maintain the conditions that the researchers deemed necessary.

As Stone and Powell arrived at the settlement, they could see that Jeff Harper was standing in front of the tiny general store that supported the community. He waved to them as they parked, and then he led them down a narrow footpath to his office and laboratory.

Once they were settled in his small office, they began to question him.

"I'm positive, Sheriff Stone, that it was Clancy himself that took a shot at me one evening when I went up to take a look at the Kebler Pass Project," the young scientist told them.

"I remember the complaint," Stone recalled. "Never did hear though, why you filed and then withdrew."

"Well, sir, I went to see Judge Winfield about suing Clancy, and he told me that I didn't have a leg to stand on. Seems Clancy had plenty of 'No Trespassing' signs posted. Winfield told me to consider myself lucky if Big Jim didn't take me to court; and like a fool, I listened to him."

"Sounds like you got some bad advice, Harper, a shooting is a shooting...especially within the city limits."

"That's just it, Sheriff. I found out that the Kebler Pass Project is outside of the limits. It would have taken me more money than I could afford to hire a good lawyer to fight Big Jim Clancy. I let it drop, but I decided I would have it out in court with him someday."

Sheriff Stone looked hard at the young scientist and asked, "Just what did you intend to do?"

"I found out through a friend of mine who works for the State's Attorney General that Clancy and Wilson never did file the required permits with the Environmental Division. In fact, I telephoned Jasper Wilson Thursday night and asked him if he could get together with me to discuss the matter before I approached Clancy about it."

"What did Wilson have to say?" Powell asked eager to hear the answer.

"Told me there must have been some kind of mistake. Said Clancy had done the papers sometime back even before Wilson committed his money to the deal."

"Didn't seem upset then?" Stoned inquired.

"Not at all. He almost sounded sympathetic to my plight. You know, sort of patronizing. He's a good man," Harper added then shook his head.

"Well, Harper, we won't take anymore of your time for now," the Sheriff spoke as he and his deputy stood to leave. "Got to be heading back into Crested Butte for a big softball game."

"I didn't know you played, Sheriff Stone."

"I play at it. Been holding down first base all season for the new Hummers' team."

"Great! I'll see you over at the game. I'm a friend of Kate Mason's and I try to support her efforts. Still haven't figured out which of the city fathers talked her into sponsoring a team, but she did tell me it gives her a tax break as an advertising expense."

"The way we've been playing, can't be too good for the store's image." Stone lamented.

The men said good-bye to each other, and the lawmen returned to their jeep. As they prepared to leave Gothic, Stone asked Powell, "How'd you like those Ropers he was wearing?"

"I liked them a lot, Boss. I particularly liked them because they were much smaller than the ones we're looking for."

"Good eye, Powell. We can put Harper on the back burner for the time being."

⌁∼

The bleachers at the public park filled up early. Deputy Powell was glad he had been able to get a good seat. He spent nearly as much time watching the crowd as he did watching the game on the field.

Tim Powell was particularly interested in observing Kate Mason and her companion, Jeff Harper. If there were not such an obvious age difference between the two, Powell would have mistaken them for a couple on a date. Not that they were displaying overt signs of affection, but there was definitely something special about the way they talked together, almost as if they were trying very hard not to be overheard.

From where he sat, Powell knew that he would never be able to overhear them anyway. Remorsefully, he wished that he had taken a lip reading class. Once or twice he noticed that they both seemed to be staring at him, and for some reason that made him uncomfortable. He assumed that Harper was telling her all about their earlier visit.

Finally, the game was over: Slogar Sluggers 6, Hummers 3.

Powell was just getting up to go down to the dugout and join the Sheriff when he noticed how the petite Kate Mason looked in the harsh lighting of the playing field lights. Her hair seemed to be aglow, not the dull brown he had previously thought it to be. He glanced away from her and toward his boss just in time to see that Stone had also made the same discovery.

8

Wednesday morning Sheriff Stone and Deputy Powell got to work early. They had both been so tired after the game the night before that they had done little more than speculate on the developments of the Clancy case during the drive back to Gunnison. The morning had been quite another matter as they had both arrived refreshed and looking forward to tackling the business at hand. More than ever, they were curious about Kate Mason and her relationship with Dr. Harper. They agreed that they needed a considerable amount of background on the lady if they were ever going to make any headway.

Another problem that they were encountering was the fact that there still had been no sign of Buck Hayden nor his pal, Ben Peek. They had just about given up hope and trying to find a new angle when they received a dispatch from the Colorado Highway Patrol. Buck Hayden's VW van had been involved in an accident during the night.

"It's Hayden's van all right," the Sheriff told Powell. "He turned it over near Grand Junction during a downpour. Went right through a barricade and caught fire."

"Were both he and Peek in the van, Boss?"

"Doesn't look that way. According to this report, the driver was badly burned and taken to the hospital. They haven't been able to get an ID yet. Description, what they've got of one, could fit either one of them. No wallet found at the scene."

"That's rough. Is the guy going to make it?" the young man queried.

"Likely he will. In spite of the burns, and being knocked out, he's got a good chance of pulling through. We'll get their findings as soon as they know something. My money says it's Peek."

"How so?" Powell was puzzled.

"Buck was pretty angry when he left town. I think the truth was that Peek had taken off with their old van. Buck would be wanting something better if he were going to make a break for it. I'm guessing that he's the one that lit out with the Chavez's Bronco. He may have had that truck loaded with Clancy's stuff too, as far as that goes. He had more than one way of getting even for being fired."

"You think he killed Big Jim?"

"That we won't know for awhile. We'll need to see if he has any of the stolen goods, then check his footprint against the cast that we've got."

"He certainly had motive and opportunity," the deputy added.

"If it had been a knifing, I'd think it was more likely. As things stand, though, there's no changing the fact that he was shot with a small caliber handgun. The kind of gun a lady might hide in her purse or keep at home for protection."

The deputy looked at his superior, and then he offered, "I imagine you will want to know if any of the women on our list have registered .22s."

"Powell, you're becoming a mind reader."

Sheriff Stone's secretary buzzed him from the outer office. "There's a Mrs. Aikens here to see you, sir. She's Jim Clancy's housekeeper, and she says she's got that inventory you requested."

"Send her in," Stone replied quickly.

⌣∶∾

By the time Sheriff Stone had finished going over the list with the housekeeper, he was tired. He was impressed by how thorough the woman had been, and he made a special effort to tell her how much he appreciated her cooperation. It was not every citizen who would take the time and the energy to put together such a comprehensive list. She had even noted the breakage and spoilage of the items.

What Stone was really after, however, were the big ticket items on her list. The kind of merchandise that could be sold or fenced. Maybe a local pawn shop could add some leads based on the list. Stone knew that if he could trace some of the stolen goods, he might get a lead to the killing. He also was experienced enough to know that the robbery might be totally independent of the murder.

The tracker looked over the accounting of the articles. Quickly memorizing the outstanding entries, Stone placed the paper in the Clancy folder. He was preparing to have his secretary send Powell back to his office when the young lawman appeared at the open doorway.

"Boss, we're running a trace on the gun registrations. Should be in any minute."

"That's good. Should shed a little light. Maybe we can at least eliminate some of the women folk we've got."

"Speaking of women, why don't we pay another visit to Mrs. Wilson? Shake her up a little. I'll get that cigarette from Property," the young man said.

"Good idea, but I think we'll ask her to come here. That will give her a chance to stew some. Also, it may be helpful to hear what she has to say when Jasper Wilson is not around." He paused then added, "By the way, did their story check that they were at the V.F.W. bingo Friday night?"

"Yes, sir, it did. The man in charge said he remembered them arriving early. Mrs. Wilson has her favorite lucky seat near the front of the room. She likes plenty of space to spread out her markers and papers."

"Markers and papers?" the older man questioned.

"That's right, Boss. They don't use bingo cards anymore."

"Man, I am dating myself now, Powell. When I played bingo years ago, we used bands or kernels of corn to cover up the numbers that had been called. I went in a fancy bingo parlor once down on an Indian reservation years ago, and they were using cards that had little window boxes a person could slide to cover numbers. But, markers?"

"The cards aren't cards anymore. Basically, they are the same design but are printed on paper that's like newsprint. Heck, they can print strips of three or even six cards a sheet for people to play. Then they've got these fat markers of a dozen colors or so that they dot onto the paper as the numbers are called."

"Powell, that doesn't sound too bad except for one thing. What happens if you accidentally mark the wrong thing? There's no way to erase that stuff, is there?"

"I guess you make an 'X' through it. I don't know, Boss," frustration edged the deputy's voice.

"Ah, well, so we've got Miss Voni playing right in the front row. What did the guy have to say about Jasper?"

"Jasper apparently always sits in the back by the door. He likes to step out for fresh air on occasion. Public restrooms across the park there are clean and never very crowded either. Hard to keep a former cattleman penned up, I imagine."

"Probably. Jasper doesn't actually play. He may be there to keep his wife company."

"You mean check up on her?" the deputy asked with a bit of surprise.

"Jasper's older than her, and he might be a bit jealous. Guess we can probe on that matter when she comes in later. What do you say we take a little look see around town and stop at the Quarter Circle for lunch?"

"I could go for some of their barbecue," the younger man agreed.

∽:∾

In Crested Butte Kate Mason worked in her little shop. She waited on a customer and wrapped his purchase very carefully. Her hired help, a young college girl on summer vacation, busily dusted the precious ornaments and crystal creatures. Kate showed the customer to the door and looked around Hummers with a measure of satisfaction. The place was really looking first rate, she acknowledged. It seemed more like an aviary than a store. The quality of the specimens Kate sold were life-like and colorful. She realized that there probably was not another store in all of Colorado that specialized in hummingbirds the way she did, and that thought encouraged her.

She appreciated the fact that she had been able to meet the well-known painter, Lisa Ridgley. Posters and paintings by Ridgley adorned the walls of Hummers. Somehow, the local artist had managed to capture the beauty of not only the hummingbirds on canvas, but also the landscape of wildflowers. Ridgley's 1989 official poster for the city's wildflower festival was Kate's favorite in the collection. It looked perfect in Hummers.

As she picked up a dust cloth to help her employee, Kate Mason suddenly became apprehensive about what would become of her collection eventually. The building itself did not matter to her even though she had transformed it from a run-down house to a fully viable business with living quarters. What concerned her most was what would become of the paintings and the little birds. For a brief awful moment, she had a mental picture of Jeff Harper liquidating the stock "garage-sale" fashion.

Kate put the cloth back and went into her office to telephone Harper. She had an idea about what she wanted him to do when she was gone.

༺ ༒ ༻

Yvonne Mason was waiting in the Sheriff's outer office when Stone and Powell returned. She looked as though she had just come from the beauty shop, her thick dark hair curled and teased out in all directions. She wore skintight, white slacks that revealed more curves than a road map, and a red, low cut sweater showed cleavage neither of the men had noticed before. She was what Stone's grandmother might have referred to as "all gussied up" from her large, dangling, red plastic earrings to her spiked high-heeled red sandals. Powell heard Stone take a deep breath as he walked over to the woman.

Soon the three of them were seated in Stone's office.

"Want to thank you for coming in," the Sheriff began.

"No trouble at all, Sheriff Stone. Any concerned citizen would be happy to help," she spoke almost coquettishly.

Powell, sitting across the room and slightly behind Mrs. Wilson, caught Stone's attention and made an exaggerated effort to roll his eyes up in mock disbelief.

"Now, Mrs. Wilson, we'd..."

"Voni, please. Everybody calls me Voni," she insisted.

"Yes, ma'am," the Sheriff continued. "As you know, we are working on the Clancy case, trying to tie up a few loose ends and thought you might be able to shed some light on a couple of matters."

"Me? Why, I don't see what I could possibly tell you that could help," she spoke softly and appeared to actually flutter her eyelashes for a second or two. "If there's anything to be told about Clancy, my husband's the one who knows......knew him best, seeing how they were partners in business and all."

"We do plan on talking to Mr. Wilson soon, ma'am, but some

of the questions we wanted to ask you might be better answered in private for the moment," he directed his statement and his gaze at the woman.

Suddenly alert, Yvonne Wilson stopped smiling. "What sort of private questions, Sheriff?"

Powell noticed there was nothing seductive about the woman's attitude; at once, she was on the defense.

Stone hesitated just long enough for the tension to build between them before he asked, "Were you with Jim Clancy the day he died?"

A look of relief crossed her face, and she relaxed. "No, sir. I did not see Big Jim on Friday."

"But you were out at his cabin?" he continued.

"How did you?..." she sounded startled.

"Were you there, ma'am?"

"Ah, let me see," she said reluctantly. "I have been out to that cabin on occasion. Big Jim's had my husband and I out there for supper a time or two. Been ages, though, since..." her voice trailed off as Deputy Powell placed the plastic bag containing her cigarette on the big desk in front of her.

Stone told her, "We have reason to believe this is yours. It was found at the cabin early Saturday and could not have been there more than twenty-four hours considering the rain of last Friday morning."

"All right. All right. I was out to the cabin. I was supposed to meet Big Jim there about six. He said he had some money he could loan me. I was a little short and wanted to make a payment to a fellow I owed in Vegas. Nothing big, you understand. Just a couple of hundred Jasper wouldn't be too happy to know about. I waited as long as I could. Stood down there by the water and smoked a cigarette, but I couldn't wait forever. Had to get home and finish getting ready to go to bingo. It starts at 7:30, and I like to get there early."

"You didn't go in the cabin?"

"Heavens no! I don't have a key or anything. As a matter of fact, I didn't feel like hanging around there. The woods always give me the creeps. Besides, like I said, I needed to get on home. Since Jasper had taken my new Blazer to work, I was stuck with his old car, and I did not want to end up stranded out there in such a spooky place. No telling what could happen to a defenseless woman all alone out there. Right then, I was wishing I had my..." she stopped herself from continuing.

"Did you have any idea at the time why Clancy hadn't shown up?" Stone inquired.

"Oh, sure. For one thing the man was very unreliable, especially if he had been drinking. He seemed to be doing a lot of that lately. And I know for a fact, he often stopped on the way home from working at the project."

"Stopped to drink?" the Sheriff sounded perplexed as he knew there were no bars along the highway between Crested Butte and Almont.

"No. He'd pull into the Roaring Judy. We've fished with him a few times out there. Claimed he would stop there and catch his dinner. Could have fished out the backdoor of his cabin if he wanted to, but he had a special fondness for that stretch of the East River. Went there as a child, I think he mentioned."

"That about does it for us, ma'am. Like I told you before, we appreciate your cooperation. There's one other little matter I'd like you to do before you leave today."

"Of course, Sheriff Stone," she agreed.

Yvonne Wilson looked very surprised when Stone said, "Please go with Deputy Powell down to the Investigation Room and let the officers there take an impression of your shoe."

The Sheriff turned to the young officer and said, "And Powell, you get yourself on back here after you help Mrs. Wilson."

Sheriff Stone watched the two of them go down the hall and wait for the elevator. As the elevator doors opened, Chris Rawlins stepped off to allow the others on. Chris was carrying a VCR under his arm and a grim look on his face.

43

9

Chris Rawlins followed the Sheriff back to his office. As they entered the room, Chris hesitated a moment, then placed the video player on the wide desk in front of the lawman.

"Says Clancy on it plain as day, son. Where'd you get it?" he was too tired to interrogate.

"Sheriff Stone, you have got to believe me. I had nothing to do with Clancy's murder. I don't know how he got the VCR. I haven't done anything; I swear!"

"Hold it! One thing at a time. No one is accusing you of anything. Now, I am mighty curious how you came into possession of this stolen property," the big man leveled his question at the youth.

"Stolen! Oh, no. I knew it. I should have known it. I'm such a stupid fool! Too good to be true." he whined and was near tears.

"We are not getting anywhere like this, Chris," he admonished. "Where did you get the VCR?"

"I bought it early Saturday morning as I was getting off the night shift at the Quik-Shop. I didn't know it was Clancy's, I swear."

"I asked you where you bought it," Stone tried to focus on the issue.

"That's what I was telling you. I bought it right there in the parking lot of the store. He was parked next to my car and was just going in to get a cup of coffee when he saw me. We talked, and I gave him my last fifty bucks for the thing."

"This guy was somebody you knew? A local?" the officer was giving the young man his full attention.

"Well, I didn't recognize his truck at first, had a big Bronco, not the van he usually drives. As soon as he said hello, I knew him right off. It was Buck Hayden."

"You're sure?" Stone asked and inhaled deeply.

"Yes, sir. He had that truck plumb full of things to sell, but I had no idea he had taken them from Clancy. I said something about all the stuff, and he said he was on his way to the flea market down at Lake City. Said I was helping him out by lightening his load in advance. Electric gear is hard to sell at those markets. People are skeptical that the electric parts are in good shape."

"He was probably telling the truth on the flea market. Could have dumped the whole load there that morning. Sure would give him plenty of cash," Stone spoke thoughtfully.

"He seemed so nice to me that morning, Sheriff. Said he had heard about the way Clancy had tossed me out of the tavern. Acted as though he was genuinely happy to see me and give me such a good deal. Wasn't until I was hooking the thing up later that I saw Clancy's engraving."

"That had to have been a few days back, son. Why didn't you come forward sooner?" the officer studied the youngster.

"I dunno. Guess I was scared you wouldn't believe me. Also, I was out the money for the machine."

"At least you did the right thing now. Your conscience can be clear. Those circles under your good eye tell me you haven't been sleeping all that much. Am I right?"

"Haven't slept at all. I was worried that you might think that I killed Clancy and took his property."

"I know you didn't kill him, son. I've talked to the Quik-Shop manager, and you were at work when the murder took place. No way could you have done it," he reassured the Rawlins boy. "There is one thing I would like you to do for me. Stop at my secretary's desk and give her your statement so she can type it up. Sign it before you leave. In fact, while you wait, why don't you go to our personnel office and apply for the clerk/dispatcher position that's just opened up. It's the same rotten hours as your job at Quik-Shop, but it pays considerable more. College kid like you could handle it."

"Thank you, Sheriff Stone. I appreciate the chance, but I will have to give the manager two weeks notice to be fair."

"I figured that. No problem. Maybe we'll see you on board here even sooner. Now hightail it on out there and get to work on that statement," he ordered the smiling youngster out of his office.

While Stone stood in his doorway, he was reminded by his secretary that he had an appointment with Judge Winfield in fifteen minutes. Powell still wasn't back from escorting Mrs. Wilson, so Stone decided not to wait. He left the building and drove to Winfield's office behind the Courthouse.

Sheriff Stone was greeted at Winfield's by the effervescent Miss Marva Lee Linden. Miss Linden had been the Judge's secretary for longer than anyone could remember. As lively as she was elderly, she seemed to know everyone's private business as well. No one told Marva Lee anything they would not want to hear repeated at the beauty shop or the grocery store within the week.

Stone wondered how she could work in a position that required a certain amount of confidentiality. Yet, to his knowledge, there had never been a time when any of the Winfield clients had complained about any impropriety by her. On the other hand, Winfield had had dozens of complaints filed against him for one reason or another.

Miss Linden apologized for Winfield's tardiness. She told Stone that he was with a client and then she offered the officer a cup of coffee before returning to her duties. While Stone waited, he glanced at a magazine or two that were on the table in front of the sofa. He was just about to call it quits and return to his own office when Deputy Powell joined him.

"It's about time you got here," the older man said sourly. "Couldn't tear yourself away from Miss Exotic?"

"Nothing like that, Boss, although it did take longer than I thought to make the shoe print. They wanted a footprint too, and you never heard such tickled giggling. Man, oh, man. She really is something else!"

"You got the print?"

"Yes, sir. Not a match. Her foot is a size or two larger than the casting."

Miss Linden had stopped typing and was actively listening to what the two men had to say. She did not want to miss a thing.

Finally, when she could not stand it any longer, she entered the conversation. "Excuse me, Sheriff, for butting in and all."

The lawmen looked up to see what she wanted.

"Couldn't help hearing you talk about someone exotic. Figure it has to be Voni Wilson, a prime suspect no doubt in the

Clancy case?"

"Ma'am, I don't believe this is..." Stone started to put her off the track and change the subject.

"Stone, I could tell you a thing or two about that woman. I have most certainly been expecting her to get herself in trouble what with her carryings on and such," she spoke smugly.

Deputy Powell interrupted, "Miss Linden, we certainly would appreciate any information you could give us. I know you are terribly busy and all, but if you could make the time...I know that I for one would be happy to sit down with you and hear more about Mrs. Wilson." He looked slyly at his boss. Powell knew Stone would be in no mood to talk to the gossipy old woman, yet, he also knew that the Sheriff would want any pertinent information.

The Sheriff smiled at him with a look that said "thanks" and "no thanks" at the same time. He would be happy to let the younger man interview the talkative snoop. He was more concerned about meeting with Winfield.

As Stone glanced up at the prim Miss Marva Lee, he was struck by the fact that he never before really looked at her. It was as though he were seeing her for the first time. Although he had sat in the Judge's office many times, he realized that not once had he actually observed the woman. That fact bothered him as he prided himself on his keen sense of observation. Looking at her working at her typewriter, he noticed how very white her hair had become. She was really starting to show her age, but she still held down a productive full time job. He began to wonder if maybe he had judged her too harshly.

"Miss Linden, if you are free after work, I hope you will let my deputy and I buy you some pie and coffee over at the W-Cafe." The Sheriff offered the invitation while smiling at the startled deputy's face.

"Why, Sheriff Stone, I'd be delighted. Shall we say fiveish?" she asked.

"That'd be fine, ma'am. If I'm running late, Powell here will get on over there and hold a booth for us. Right, deputy?"

"Yes, sir. Place crowds up about then, so I'll get there early."

Marva Lee took a call on the intercom, then told the Sheriff that he could go on into Winfield's inner office.

Jeff Harper walked along the shore of the Oh-Be-Joyful Creek just outside of Crested Butte. He wanted some time alone to think. He was becoming more and more concerned about his friend, Kate Mason. The woman had always been somewhat of a mystery to him, but the last few days, her behavior had perplexed him even more.

Harper cherished his friendship with Kate Mason. She was a woman unlike any other he had ever met. She had a terrific sense of humor and was very intelligent; she seemed to be always studying or reading something to learn about new ideas. With all of her vitality and zest for life, he could not understand why she had so suddenly started talking about death and dying and wills.

Harper knew that he spent too much time worrying about her. After all, he told himself, she was practically old enough to be his mother. If not his mother, then the fifteen years difference in their ages would make her more like an older sister. He realized that he did not think she looked like anybody's older anything. She was just too youthful and pretty to be in her forties. For a moment he wondered if she were lying about her age, but then he told himself that most women who lie about their ages do it to seem younger, not older.

After a few minutes he spotted a fallen tree trunk near the water's edge, and he sat down and began tossing small gravel pebbles into the Oh-Be-Joyful. He watched the little rocks enter the swirling waters and wondered how many miners had panned those same pebbles looking for gold nuggets. As he thought about the miners and their dreams of riches, his mind turned once again to Kate's will. He knew at that moment he did not want to be her beneficiary. He wanted her to live for a very long time.

10

Judge Grant Winfield reminded Tim Powell of Jabba the Hutt. Winfield was grossly overweight and appeared to the deputy as though he were wider than the chair under him. The large man's stomach seemed to fold out over his belt in such a grotesque manner, that Powell was momentarily sickened at the sight. The younger man believed that he had finally figured out the reason why the Judge was seldom seen out of his official robes before he returned to private practice; the robes could hide a multitude of sins.

At once, Powell returned his attention to the present conversation that was taking place between the Sheriff and Winfield.

"Now, Sheriff," the large man drawled slowly. "I don't mean to suggest that you would be going off half cocked at all. I just fail to see where that type of questioning is leading." He scowled at the lawman.

"Well, sir, we are developing some theories now, and I really wish you would make the records available. I can get a court order if you insist," Stone spoke politely but firmly.

"Naw, that won't be necessary," he mumbled. "It'll be all over the papers soon enough. Clancy's failure to file properly is going to halt the work at Kebler Pass. Wilson himself told me that another work stoppage would put them under. With the short construction season they have up there at that altitude, there is no way the framing in can get done before winter. That means a year delay at the site. Neither Clancy nor Wilson could ride out a financial storm like that."

"Are you positive, Winfield? I understood that their company was more solvent than that," the Sheriff continued probing.

"Clancy had plenty of money. He has, or rather, had holdings

49

all over this county. He might have propped up the operation if he had lived. It will all be in Probate now," he added remorsefully.

"What about Wilson? Is this going to wipe him out?"

" 'Fraid so. He put up his ranch against the note. Must be a real blow to him to see everything collapse like that. Course, he still has some property in town and part interest in a venture or two. Small potatoes really."

As the lawmen rose to leave the man, Sheriff Stone turned to ask one more question.

"You and Jim Clancy went way back, didn't you?"

The fat man's eyes narrowed cautiously as he replied. "We were friendlies for a long time."

"Friendlies? Not friends?" Stone asked.

"We were acquainted, Sheriff, but we did not socialize. Never had much in common."

Sheriff Stone stared at the man, but he did not pursue the questioning. One thing Sheriff Stone was good at and he knew it, was recognizing a lie when he heard one.

༺༻

At Crested Butte, the hummingbirds swirled frantically in jewel-like colors seeking additional nectar for the cold night ahead. Having completed their 1500-mile journey from Mexico, the broadtailed males preened and dove before the females they attempted to enchant during the feasting. Rich with larkspur, the East River Valley was the perfect territory for the hungry migrants. As they flit from flower to flower, their iridescent feathers sparkled in the late afternoon sun.

Maneuvering from blossom to blossom, their tiny bodies appeared immobile and suspended, nearly hidden among the red columbine and Indian paintbrush. Fueling their powerful metabolism with feedings every twenty minutes, they barely had time for the purpose of nature that had compelled them to the upper reaches of the Rocky Mountains.

༺༻

Stone and Powell returned to the Sheriff's office long enough to make a few telephone calls and pick up a report. Stone was able to phone the team captain of the Hummers to let him know that he would not be available to play the following night. Powell looked over the memo from Gun Registration and was interested to note that both Kate Mason and Yvonne Wilson owned .22s. He brought that fact to the Sheriff's attention at once. Later, the two officers drove to the W-Cafe to await Miss Linden.

The W-Cafe was as smokey and crowded as ever. The locals were already packed into the restaurant on Main Street and busy ordering slices of homemade pie and other delectables from the menu as the officers arrived. Stone understood why the townsfolk found the place so attractive; the prices were reasonable and the food was delicious. It was a winning combination that kept the cafe popular from season to season. It was the kind of restaurant that appealed to the hunter and to the fisherman as well as to the local businessmen. Shoppers paused there long enough to recharge their batteries before going back out on the street.

The two men were able to find a vacant booth along the far side of the big room. They counted themselves fortunate as the booth would afford a measure of privacy for their discussion with Miss Linden. As they glanced around the restaurant and sipped on the water the waitress had left with them, they noticed that there seemed to be a lot of unfamiliar faces in the gathering.

"Looks like the summer folks are starting to arrive for the Balloon Fiesta," the older man remarked to his partner. "I hardly know anyone here."

"With these uniforms, we can be sure they all recognize you. I would hate for us to have to do any undercover work in this town. Can you imagine the disguises we'd have to come up with to blend in?"

"That reminds me, when is our trip to the beauty parlor?"

"Oh, Boss," the deputy moaned. "I thought those pictures of the hair frosting business did the trick."

"Yes, Powell. I was just kidding. Kate Mason seems the obvious candidate for the hair sample test. I still wish we knew a little more about her."

"I'll get a message up to Vail first thing. I know she came here from there. Who knows? Maybe it will turn out that she is a serial killer or something." Powell mused.

"Don't go jumping off the deep end. Remember you are speaking about the sponsor of my own team, such as it is," he sounded regretful.

The deputy called Stone's attention to the fact that Linden had just entered the cafe. They both slid out of the booth and stood waiting while she made her way through the crowd to join them.

"This is nice," Miss Linden remarked as she sat with the men. "Got this nice young fellow here by my side and the Sheriff of the County across from me, why I feel safe indeed," she told them happily.

Stone told her, "We're just pleased that you agreed to meet with us. If you feel it's too crowded, we could go somewhere else."

"Oh, no, Sheriff. In all this noise, no one is going to overhear a thing. I believe I can speak freely."

She prepared to tell them something, but hesitated until the waitress had come and gone with their orders.

"As I mentioned at Winfield's, I do have some meaty facts about Voni Wilson. I have known that girl since she was a teenager. Her folks moved in next to me over on Georgia Street. To tell you the truth, I have never met a more selfish or back talking little girl than her. I swear she gave her folks grey hair and early graves. They never could control her."

"What did she do?" Powell asked.

"What didn't she do would be more like it." the lady answered. "She stayed out 'til all hours of the night. You know she was an only child and spoiled rotten to start with. She dressed like a million dollars, though. Always had her nails polished and wore more makeup than was decent for a girl her age. One boyfriend after another would be parked in her driveway until nearly daylight. I can't repeat some of the things I saw that young woman doing in those cars. You know my window looks smack dab down on their drive."

"Sounds like a willful child, but that doesn't necessarily make her a suspect in a murder case," Stone reminded her.

"I was just getting to that. Wasn't until she was barely out of high school that the rumor was that she was pregnant. Her folks were beside themselves when they told me about it. Seems Jasper Wilson was a friend of theirs and offered to marry the girl and give the baby a name. Jasper had plenty of money and a nice ranch, and he had admired her looks from afar. He was several years older than her, and her parents thought that he might be able to settle her down some. Before anyone knew it, they were married."

Powell questioned, "I don't recall that they have any children."

"They don't," she answered smuggly. "Voni went off to some clinic in Denver, and when she came back, there was no baby and no more pregnancies."

"Sad for Jasper Wilson, I guess," Stone replied thinking of the joy his own son gave him.

"Voni has always been one step ahead of her husband. I don't know if she ever wanted to marry him or not, but she took full advantage of his money. I think they were doing OK though, until Big Jim came into the picture."

"Big Jim?" the younger man asked.

"It's common knowledge that on occasion Voni has run up some sizeable gambling debts. Clancy's money has bailed her out a time or two; I will leave it to you gentlemen to imagine how she was repaying those debts to Jim Clancy." Marva Lee pursed her thin lips.

"Excuse me, Miss Linden," Powell queried. "How do you know about Clancy and Mrs. Wilson's...arrangement."

"Why through Judge Winfield, of course. I heard the two of them laughing about it in Winfield's office one evening when they thought I had already left and gone home. Believe me, officers, I wouldn't tell you anything that I did not know to be a fact." She said proudly.

Stone decided to change the subject somewhat and question the secretary about the relationship between Winfield and Clancy.

"Thick as thieves! Probably thieving too," she replied. "Those two have been in cahoots for a very long time; but for the life of me, I haven't figured out what it is. I have tried," she assured the officers.

Sheriff Stone tried to picture Marva Lee Linden as a real detective, but could not conjure up an image.

"I do not know how it all started, but Winfield used to make monthly payments to Clancy. I assumed it was some kind of blackmail, but eventually the payments stopped, and Clancy started coming to the office. He was always cordial, but I felt that there was something sneaky going on. The Judge allowed him in no matter what the appointment book said." She caught her breath and took a sip of water. "If you ever figure out what was going on between those two, Sheriff, I would be interested in knowing."

Sheriff Stone smiled at the lady and told himself that he did not doubt that for a moment.

53

11

Thursday morning Sheriff Stone woke up earlier than usual. The sun was streaming in so brightly through the bedroom window that it woke him an hour before his alarm was set to ring. He decided to take advantage of the time and go for an early morning jog. Dressing quietly in order not to disturb his wife, he slipped into his sweats and went downstairs to have a glass of juice before hitting the road. He walked past his son's room and smiled as he looked in on the slumbering boy.

Leaving by the kitchen door, Stone started up the incline path that led to the campus of Western State College. He realized at once that he was beginning to get out of shape as he huffed his way up the side street to the main campus. There was one thing he did regret about his softball team, they never seemed to get enough exercise. Mostly, they stood around.

As he made his way toward Escalante Drive along the campus perimeter, Stone noticed that there were still traces of low hanging clouds and mists down the slopes of the nearby peaks. He assumed that the temperature during the night must have been much lower than he first supposed. He exhaled forcefully and saw his own breath in the cool moist air.

He was glad that he had cancelled out of the ball game. He decided that he needed to spend an evening with his family. It was not so bad, he concluded, when the night games were in town, but when they were away in Crested Butte, it did create a hardship for the family now that his son had a summer job with the Parks and Recreation Department. He accepted the fact that his son was growing up and only had one year of high school left, but that did not make it any easier. Frank Stone loved his child and dreaded the day the boy would feel he needed to leave home.

As he ran downhill along the eastern side of the campus, he reached the Aspinall-Wilson Center. The attractive structure caught his eye, and he slowed down at the parking lot and turned to look across the green lawns at the major buildings of the college. He doubted that he had ever seen a more pleasant institution of higher learning. Granted, it was a very small college, but he wondered if there were many other schools that could offer the quality in academics and the proximity to the ski slopes. He determined to mention those facts to his son later that evening. With any luck, he thought, he might be able to convince his boy to at least consider attending Western State.

Stone ran on down Georgia Avenue and then turned toward his home. Glancing at his watch, he noted that he still had time to shower and dress and be at work early. He took a deep breath and began to sprint the last few yards to his house.

꒳:꒳

Jasper Wilson left home early for the Kebler Pass Project site. As he drove along Highway 135 from Gunnison, he decided to stop at the Almont Resort for breakfast. As he arrived at the Three Rivers area, he parked the new Blazer under a cluster of pines that made up the cleared parking area of the restaurant and cottages.

The pine-paneled dining room was crowded, but he was able to find a small table by the large picture windows that looked out on the parking lot and across the road to the cabins that were close to the water. He could see the edge of the small road that led down to Clancy's cabin, and for a moment, he allowed himself to remember some of the good times he had shared with Big Jim in the earlier days of their partnership.

While he stared out of the window, he was momentarily distracted by the arrival of three hummingbirds to the hanging feeders outside the window. He could not recall having ever seen three birds at one feeder before, so he watched them in fascination.

Each of the three birds was different. One was a somewhat dull shade with yellow glints of color showing when it hovered alongside the red and white feeder. It seemed to be the smallest and most nervous of the three as it darted to the feeder then quickly flew to a nearby spruce and hid. It seemed to wait and watch while

55

the other two chased and played tag next to the glowing red globe of sugared water.

If the two brightly colored creatures were even aware of the third one, they did not give any sign of noticing or caring as they stood on the tiny perches of the feeder. As they took in the sweet waters, they darted from place to place. Always alert, their little bodies were seldom still. As the waitress approached Jasper Wilson's table, her image in the window startled the birds, and they flew away instantly, leaving the man alone at the table to contemplate what he had seen.

⌒:∾

Frank Stone was in his office and hard at work before anyone else arrived. He left a note on his secretary's desk that he was not to be disturbed until nine o'clock unless it was an emergency. He also asked for her to let Powell know he wanted to see him at 9:30.

Stone wanted no distractions as he prepared to make a chart for himself. He planned to lay out all of the information that he had accumulated on the the Clancy Case and to try and make some kind of sense and order out of the facts. As he spread out the large sheets of paper across the wide desk, he began to write:

Who—Jim W. Clancy
What—Murder Victim
When—Friday at approximately 7pm.
Where—on the west bank of the East River, south of the Roaring Judy.
How—a single shot from a .22 pistol. Shot at close range.
Why—?
By whom—?

Stone left the last two categories blank as he continued making entries on his chart:

Other factors—Blood alcohol level, .11, legally drunk.
     Two shoe prints at the scene, a lady's size six,
     and a Roper size 10.
     Woman's hair found on Clancy's shirt.

Next, he ruled off sections on his paper and began to summarize what he had on each suspect. He was not entirely certain why he did it, but he began with the name, Kate Mason.

Ms. Kate Mason, background unknown but claims to be Denver/Vail. Owner of the Hummers in Crested Butte. Fits the size suggested by the shoe print, but has not had her foot measured yet. Hair found at the scene could be hers, also, fits the description. She was seen there by the ranger. Has a .22 pistol registered in her name.

Sheriff Stone looked at the last and probably most damaging entry. He added to the list that there was no known motive for her to have wanted to kill the man. In fact, she and Clancy seemed to have been on friendly terms, perhaps even socializing. He recalled the note at the cabin that indicated that Clancy was to see the Mason woman later that night. Stone would ask Powell later if there had been word from Vail. All in all, he could not picture Kate Mason as a murderer. He considered that perhaps the shooting had been accidental, and the woman might be too frightened to come forward.

Stone turned his attention to the next name on his list, Jasper Wilson. He proceeded to jot down the facts he had on Wilson. He noted that the ranger's list placed the man's Blazer at the scene that day. Stone had noted that Wilson was a bitter, angry man. Wilson had as much as said that he was glad Clancy was dead. There was also the possibility that the man knew about his wife's dealing with Clancy.

Stone decided to get a search warrant and have ballistics take a look at the .22 owned by Mrs. Wilson. Perhaps they would uncover a pair of Ropers at the Wilson place as well. He was certain that he needed to bring Jasper Wilson in for further questioning.

The next suspect that Sheriff Stone considered was Buck Hayden. Buck was known around town to be a mean fellow with a nasty temper. He was usually just inches away from arrest. Like a bridesmaid and never a bride, Buck Hayden had been able to worm his way out of the arms of justice time after time. He usually had alibies supplied by Ben Peek. So far, very little had been pinned on Hayden until the Clancy murder; Stone felt confident that Chris Rawlins' account of buying stolen merchandise from Hayden would prove to be true. Stone had already alerted the authorities in Lake City to try and help him trace the other items from Clancy's cabin. The missing Bronco was certain to be spotted before long, and Stone was taking bets that Hayden would be found driving it. He would have his secretary check the Grand Junction hospital again for an

ID on the accident-burn victim. He had a gut feeling that it would prove to be Ben Peek.

Reflecting on the information he had on Hayden, he noted that the man had the motive and the time to do the killing. There was still no evidence, however, that he had access to the murder weapon. In any event, when Buck Hayden was brought in to custody, he would have to do a lot of explaining.

Stone continued down his list. His notations were becoming briefer as he made entries beside the names of Judge Grant Winfield, Dr. Jeff Harper, Yvonne Wilson, and finally Chris Rawlins. After a moment, he completely crossed off the Rawlins boy's name. As was his habit in his thoroughness, he constructed a separate list of names with no entries: Mrs. Aikens, Lacey Rawlins, Ben Peek, and Linden. He wondered if there was someone else? He determined to return to the Roaring Judy and see if there might have been any witnesses that day.

At 9:30 sharp, Deputy Powell tapped on his office door. Stone could tell immediately that the grinning young man had good news for him.

"It's Peek, Boss. Ben Peek's the one in the Grand Junction hospital. Now we know that Buck Hayden has the Bronco. Confirms the Rawlins kid's story too," he spoke cheerily.

"Good work, Powell. That accident puts Peek far from the county at the time of the murder, so we can at least eliminate his name from the list," he said as he stood up and leaned over his desk to cross Peek's name off the chart.

"Looks like you have been hard at it, sir," the younger man observed as he scanned the chart before them.

"I find it helps me if I can write it all out in sequence like this," he spoke as he showed the junior officer a timeline he was constructing. "I like to see the suspects' names lined up on paper too, kind of my own 'line up' without them actually being physically present. It's a matter of logic once I have all of the facts."

"That's the hard part, though, isn't it?" the officer noted. "How do we ever know when all the facts are in? What if we stop gathering evidence too soon? What if we don't have all of the pieces in the puzzle, Boss? How do we even know that we are on track?" he asked.

"Easy, Powell. That's why I've got you. Need those young brains and creative thoughts," he told the junior man then laughed aloud.

Deputy Powell was not quite certain whether the Sheriff meant the remark to be a kind one or not, but since he had noticed that Stone did not seem to have a mean bone in his entire body, he would accept the statement as a compliment at least for the time being. As far as the part about the young brains went, he knew for a fact that there was absolutely nothing wrong or defective about the older man's thought processes.

As for the youth versus age controversy, he readily accepted the knowledge that Frank Stone was in far better physical shape than he was. He was certain that Stone could outrun him in any race. The Sheriff was in tip-top condition, and his strength showed itself through the crisp uniform shirt as the powerful arms and shoulders moved in the course of the work. Powell hoped he would eventually have even a small portion of the measure of respect in the county that Stone enjoyed.

"I've got something else too, Boss," the deputy continued. "Vail PD telephoned earlier for you. Your secretary transferred the call to me."

"OK? What have they got on Mason?" he sounded eager to hear the report.

"Well, not all that much. She has had no arrests. Her sheet is totally clean. I did find out from the officer that called that Mason was a Denver widow—something we already knew, but the interesting part was that her daughter was killed there by a drunk driver last December. Seems our Kate Mason made a nuisance of herself trying to get some action on the case. She became quite a pain at their headquarters. Then, she moved away. Apparently, she came directly here from there," he speculated.

"Call them back, Powell, and ask them to send us a copy of everything they've got regarding her daughter's accident. Anything else?"

"Yeah, they told me that Kate Mason was a teacher at the local high school. She was nearing retirement, but suffered some sort of breakdown after her daughter's death. Mason took a leave of absence from the school."

"That doesn't surprise me. It would be a very traumatic thing to lose your child, no matter how many children you had, no matter how old the child was." He added thoughtfully, "You'll find out about all of this one of these days when you find the right gal and settle down with a family of your own."

For a brief moment, Deputy Powell's mind flashed back to the cute Linda Lou at the Almont Resort.

"By the way, Powell, I'm going out to the Roaring Judy after lunch."

"Want me to go along, Boss?" he asked hopefully.

"No. I need for you to stay here and hold down the fort for me. We're still waiting on an update on the Bronco APB. Also, I want to get that info on Mason as soon as we can," he instructed the younger lawman.

"Yes, sir," Powell replied.

"And one other thing...heard on the radio coming in this morning that there may be a powerful storm front pushing into the area later today or tonight. Make certain the department keeps current updates on that weather system."

12

Sheriff Stone turned off of Highway 135 and followed the gravel road that led to the Roaring Judy. He crossed over the East River Bridge and drove up in front of the building complex of the trout hatchery. There were no cars or trucks around, so he assumed that the ranger was on patrol. He hoped he would get a chance to talk to the official before he returned to Gunnison.

He drove southward past the enormous concrete holding tanks of trout of all sizes. Following the rutted road, he went beyond the tanks and the open area to a narrow lane through a forest. The road curved onward, and the Sheriff maneuvered his jeep carefully to the large, cleared field that served as a parking lot for the fishermen. He parked near the second pond, well away from the first pond and the public restroom facility.

The sun was still high in the sky and the lawman frowned to see that there was a very dark band of clouds forming along the western horizon. He wished that there were a telephone at the area, as he knew his radio would not have the range to reach his dispatcher. He considered driving back to the hatchery, but decided he could wait. He wanted to get to the crime scene and have another look before any storms hit and obliterated the location. Stone realized that any mountain rainstorm could cause a wall of water to sweep down the East River and engulf the banks.

Retracing the path he had taken the previous Friday, the Sheriff walked along the embankment between the two ponds. The ranger had posted 'No Fishing' signs along the way, so there were no other persons in the area. Ordinarily, Stone recalled, the ponds would be surrounded by fishermen and their families all trying to catch the elusive "big one."

The lawman stopped at the center of the embankment and watched a beaver moving quietly through the water at the edge of the south pond. Chipmunks popped their heads up out of their burrows, and two of them even came running toward Stone as though they were expecting him to feed them. They were obviously accustomed to having humans toss them treats.

As Frank Stone knelt to have a closer look at the woodland creatures, he thought he heard someone talking. The voice seemed to come from the direction of the river. He wondered who had managed to come into the off-limits section and how they had gotten there. Straightening up, he continued quietly along the path on the eastern edge of the pond. The reeds and grasses were so tall and dense that he could not see more than a foot or two ahead at a time. Nevertheless, he followed the sound of a man's voice.

Finally, the footpath came to an opening that led to the bank of the river. In spite of the noise of the river water, he could still hear someone speaking. He continued picking his way along the large rocks and pieces of driftwood until he saw a man standing on a wide flat rock that jutted out into the fast moving stream. The man had his back to Stone and was fly casting while speaking in a very loud voice. The Sheriff glanced around to look for the man's companion, then stopped for he suddenly recognized the fisherman, Willis Miller.

Willis Miller was well known to Sheriff Stone. On more than one occasion he had hauled Miller in for being passed out drunk behind one store or another. It always pained the lawman to have to arrest the old man, but the law was the law. Besides, there had been a couple of times in the winter, that if the patrolmen had not brought him to the jail, he certainly would have frozen to death during the night.

Miller was in his seventies and proud of the fact that he had served his country in Europe during the war. He came home from the conflict minus an arm and part of his mind; he was never right in his head after he was wounded. Stone recalled stories he had heard about Miller's heroism in battle and knew that the men to whom Miller continued to talk aloud were no longer on the earth. They had long since gone on to meet their maker.

Stone shouted at the chattering man, "Willis Miller!"

The old fellow turned around and gave a big smile to the officer. "How do, Sheriff? Ain't it a beauty of a day?" He pulled back his fishing rod and grasped the line in his hand as he greeted Stone.

The Sheriff knew that the old man, as a disabled veteran from the state of Colorado, had fishing privileges that he took full advantage of every day. He watched the old fellow step cautiously from the big rock back to the shore.

"What brings you out here, Sheriff Stone?" he asked.

The whiskey laden breath of the old man nearly turned the younger man's stomach, but he would not be his judge.

"I might ask you the same thing, but that would be foolish since I can see your rod and tackle box." He continued, "Didn't you see the posted signs? This zone is closed."

"As a matter of fact, I did see one sign, but I figured it was an old one posted for the weekend crowd. Reckon the ranger just forgot to take it down." He grinned sheepishly.

"Not quite, Miller. This whole area is off limits for a few more days. We've got a murder investigation going on here. I don't suppose you have heard anything about that either?" he chided.

"Oh, yes. Big Jim Clancy bought it right out here last Friday. I feel real bad about that. Clancy used to spend almost as much time out here as I do. Why Friday we were just having a Jack Daniels..."

"You were here Friday?" the Sheriff interrupted.

"Sure thing. I come out here most every Friday. Like I said, we were sitting right over there just tipping back and watching the water. Fish just weren't biting at all," he lamented with a sigh.

"Was there anyone else out here?" the lawman questioned. "Did you see anyone else?"

"Yes, sir, I did. I was over there behind that tree...err, relievin' myself when I heard a terrible ruckus. Clancy's partner, Jasper Wilson, was there yellin' at Big Jim something fierce. He was mighty upset, I can tell you!"

"Did you happen to hear any of the conversation?" Stone needed facts.

"I heard Big Jim call him a 'little pipsqueak,' and that's when I just burst out laughin'. They both looked over at me, and Wilson stomped off and out of here. I had to leave right after that. I always try to make it back on Friday to go to bingo." He shook his head, then added softly, "I don't recall if I went to bingo or not though.

It's a bit fuzzy."

"Thanks much, what you've told me may help. Do you have any idea what time it was when you left?"

"Must have been 6:30 or so. Wilson was still sitting in his truck when I got back to the parking lot. Man, was his face red! Poor guy's probably got high blood pressure. No sense getting himself all riled up like that. I know, I've got friends in the VA hospital messed up by that."

"Wilson was still there? You're certain?"

"Sheriff, I am as certain as my brain will allow me to be at this point. Reliable, I ain't," he remarked sadly.

Stone said good-bye to Miller and felt a great sorrow as he watched the old-timer trudge away with his gear. When the man was out of sight, he turned his attention back to the exact spot where Clancy's body had lain. The chalk marks were still visible as an outline on the rocks. There was even a faint stain that Stone tried not to notice.

⌁∿

Judge Grant Winfield wished that he had never gotten involved with Jim Clancy. He had been a fledgling lawyer just starting up a small practice in the city when he had committed a serious indiscretion. He was barely out of law school at the time, and Jim Clancy wasn't much more than a teenager himself when the trouble began, Winfield recalled, a lifetime ago.

It all happed at Irvin Lake, he remembered. He had gone out there on horseback to spend the Fourth of July weekend tenting in the forest. Several families were already camped around when he arrived. Back then, he reminisced, folks just had the basics and no frills. There were never fancy firework displays nor professional musicians. Ordinary folks just took the weekend off for the holiday celebration and pitched their tents where they could. Everybody brought his own food and a might extra to share with a neighbor.

Winfield allowed himself to relive the day in his mind. It had been a beautiful day on the Fourth. The sun dazzled the clear cool sky of the Colorado high country, and he had been feeling particularly proud of himself and the start-up of his law practice. He also had not missed the come-hither looks he was receiving from Verna Mae Curdy.

Verna was a pretty girl with dark brown hair that shined with hints of red in the sunlight. She was short and very slender with a pixie-like way of walking quickly as she helped her mother gather firewood for their campfire. She had a natural grace and an incredibly friendly smile. She also had a way of looking at Winfield that made his temperature rise.

That night after the sing-a-long, Winfield had watched the Curdy family bed down. He was feeling a little restless himself, so he decided to walk down to the lake shore. He carried a jug of "hooch" with him as he strolled through the darkness to the water's edge. Jim Clancy was already there.

Clancy and his mother had come to the lake with her brother's family. Ever since Clancy's father had died, the widow had tried her best to provide for herself and the boy. The railroad pension took care of most of the necessities but there was not much left over for luxuries or entertainment. The Fourth of July outing offered a pleasant diversion.

Jim Clancy spent most of the time being bored. There were not many children his age at the gathering, so each night he sneaked out after his mother was asleep and stole a few moments alone down by the water. He enjoyed the solitude of the quiet surroundings for he could hear the night owls and other creatures stirring in the woodland. He was simply sitting on a fallen log when Grant Winfield arrived carrying the forbidden fruit.

They sat there talking and taking turns swigging from the jug. Clancy was not as accustomed to drinking as Winfield was, but he enjoyed the fiery liquid and the lawyer's company. Not many minutes later, Verna joined them. She pretended not to see them at first, then feigned surprise that they were there. Winfield recalled that at the time both he and Clancy were sober enough to know it was all an act and that she had deliberately sought out the company.

Verna did not need much coaxing to try the strong drink they were sharing. She took a big gulp and gasped aloud, turning around quickly to see if anyone back up at the campground had heard her. They laughed and continued to drink for a half hour or so. Once, Clancy told her to slow down, but she ignored the warning telling him that she could drink anything Mr. Winfield gave her. They continued drinking and telling stories awhile longer, then the girl stood up, wobbly on her feet. She announced that she was going skinny dipping and anyone who was brave enough could join her.

Both men tried to talk her out of the idea as the temperature had dropped considerably during the time that they had been out of doors. She kept insisting, however, and faster than either of the men could imagine, she was out of her clothes and swimming in the icy waters. While they strained their eyes to watch her in the darkness, they saw her head straight out toward the center of the lake. She swam briskly at first, then disappeared from sight.

At first, neither of the men knew what to think about the disappearance. They did not know if she swam beyond their sight or whether shadows on the lake were obscuring their vision. They had both drunk so much that nothing made sense to either of them. After a time had passed, they agreed that the girl must have made it to the other side of the lake somehow. They took turns cussing the cold and the girl.

Finally, Clancy suggested that they might as well go back to bed and quit waiting on and fussing around about the foolish girl. He convinced Winfield that she had probably decided to get out of the water and walk back along the lake front. Winfield had agreed at the time, but later questioned his own sanity.

When Verna's body was found in the morning, it was determined to be a simple case of drowning. No autopsy was ever performed. Both Clancy and Winfield knew that if any tests had been done, they would have revealed the alcohol poisoning of the young girl. For years, Clancy reminded Winfield of their youthful folly and the fact that it was the "respectable Grant Winfield" who had supplied the naïve youngster.

For years, Winfield had been paying back Clancy. In the early years, he had given him small sums of money. As time went on, he had done other favors for the man in return for his silence. He knew that he would never have received the judgeship if the truth had come out. Clancy had kept his word and his mouth shut, but he had exacted a toll through the years.

Winfield was almost glad that Clancy was finally dead and off his back. He felt a particular relief that he would not be called upon to help Clancy out of any more of his legal jams. Although he did not consider himself to be a totally honorable man, he had found Clancy's last episode to be particularly distasteful and had told him as much. As far as Winfield was concerned, the incident at Vail was the last straw.

As he prepared to leave for the day, he stood by the window and watched the fast moving clouds closing in on the skies over Gunnison. He saw a distant flash of lightning and wondered if he could make it to the drugstore for some antacid before the rain hit. Clutching his ample midsection, he hurried pass Miss Linden at her desk.

13

Sheriff Stone walked closer to the river's edge and reached down into the swirling waters. The clear water was refreshingly cold. As he knelt there, he was reminded of a story he had once heard in town. It seems that there used to be an old codger in Gunnison that claimed he could put his hand in the stream, wiggle his fingers like bait, and catch fish with his bare hands.

As he watched the waters splashing and tumbling their way to the confluence of the three rivers, he listened to the soothing sounds they made. Sitting quietly, Frank Stone took the time to observe the surroundings, trying to take in each facet of the environment. From the clear blue stream to the whitish-gray rocks, to the sprigs of weeds and wildflowers, he let his gaze scan the scene. He continued looking slowly upward letting his eyes register every detail. The bushes and trees all passed under his scrutiny.

Finally, his view included the sky above, and he was somewhat surprised to see how cloudy the day had become. Brief afternoon showers were very common for the time of year, but Stone noted that the clouds were not the friendly looking puffs of white that usually preceded the rains. The storm front, he observed, seemed to be dark, tinged with a greenish hue and moving rapidly. He could tell that there would be a lot of wind accompanying the storm.

As he turned his back on the river, he felt the first cold blast of the fast moving thunderstorm. A streak of lightning illuminated the darkening sky, so he started to run toward the jeep. He reached his vehicle just as the fat drops began to fall. Safely inside the jeep, he backed up to turn and go out of the parking area; as he did so, he stopped abruptly. Through the splatter of raindrops and the smear of the windshield, he could see the ranger's official truck heading straight toward him at high speed.

The ranger honked the horn of the big 4X4 and frantically waved to the lawman. He needed to stop the officer because he had received an urgent message for the Sheriff of Gunnison County. Frank Stone's office had called the hatchery for the ranger to advise the Sheriff that there had been a serious lightning strike and that some workers from the Parks and Recreation Department had been seriously injured in Jorgensen Park.

The message hit Stone like a cold blade of steel.

༄༅

Kate Mason and Jeff Harper sat in the cozy warmth of The Bakery on Elk Avenue in Crested Butte. Because of the impending bad weather and the lack of customers, Kate had closed her store early and had telephoned Harper inviting him to join her for one of The Bakery's famous eclairs and a hot cup of coffee. He had seemed more than willing to comply with her request but insisted on paying for the refreshments.

In The Bakery, it appeared as if half of the citizens of the village had the same idea. There was a constant line of customers waiting to place orders at the counter.

"Jeff, I have been thinking about what we talked about, and I think that I would like my hummingbird collection to be donated to the Old Rock Schoolhouse. Now that the building has been totally renovated, I think there would be room for an educational display of the birds," she told him.

"Educational?" he asked, uncertain what she intended.

"Yes. I thought perhaps it would be nice for the citizens to see videotapes and maps or drawings explaining the birds' migration routes, their nests, and all of the aspects of their lives. Of course, there would be a variety of birds of different plumage also."

"Don't tell me you are considering stuffed birds as well?" he looked troubled as he asked.

"No. No. I'm thinking of asking an artist to do a set of watercolors. Don't you think that would be a fine thing to commission?" she asked the young man.

"Excellent, Kate. A wonderful idea. I should have known you would have a beautiful plan," he said as he reached across the table and took her hand.

69

She looked down at the strong young hand that held her own, and she was suddenly embarrassed to feel tears filling her eyes. Slowly and gently she withdrew from his grasp.

Seeming not to notice the woman's brief discomfort, Harper stood and picked up their coffee cups. He said, "I'll get us a refill and be right back."

She watched him make his way between the crowded tables and back to the counter. She saw him pour the refills and add milk to her cup. He knew her very well, she realized.

A loud thunderclap momentarily startled the clientele, and the lights flickered briefly. The conversations paused for a split second but resumed immediately. Everyone seemed to be enjoying the pleasant atmosphere of the eatery.

Kate Mason was particularly glad to be indoors and not out in the cold downpour. She remembered that her doctor had warned her during her last appointment that she could not afford to catch even the slightest cold.

∻

Deputy Powell waited at the front door of the headquarters building for Sheriff Stone. Stone had telephoned him from the ranger's station, but they had not had any news for him at that time. Now, as the deputy watched for the senior officer's return, he noticed how bad the rain had become, and he began to worry about Stone's safety driving in the storm.

As Powell looked out through the rain-streaked glass doors, he shuddered to think how slippery the streets would be. The patrol cars were already fully dispatched to trouble spots around the city trying to restore traffic lights at key intersections. It was obvious to him from where he stood that the pale lane marker lines of the pavement had all but vanished beneath the blowing sheets of rainwater.

He saw the headlights of the Sheriff's jeep as the man pulled into his parking stall.

Sheriff Stone rushed to the building. He was dripping wet from the rain, and he shook off the water as he came through the outer doors. Powell greeted the man with paper towels he had brought from the men's room.

Stone's voice boomed over the noise of the storm, "My son? Is my son all right?"

70

"Yes, Boss," the young officer replied. "I checked first thing. He was not with that crew today."

Greatly relieved, the Sheriff continued, "The others? How bad are they hurt?"

"Two of them are over at the hospital, mostly shaken up. I heard that one guy's zipper was fused, but you know how stories go. Everyone else was seen in the emergency room then released."

"We can be thankful that things weren't any worse than that. It's really nasty out there right now," he remarked. "What's the weather update? Is this going to last long?"

Powell told him what he had heard, "This is just the front edge of the storm, sir. Looks like it's packing even higher winds for later in the night."

"That's not good. Have we got everyone out on the street?"

"Yes, sir, except for the skeleton crew and us, all units are out there or on call."

"Get a message out to all of them. I want them to rotate back in here one unit at a time as soon as possible. Get Supply to issue every car a chain saw until we run out of them. If there is going to be a big blow, there are bound to be a lot of limbs down. I want the streets kept as free as possible for the emergency and city crews. Gonna be a lot of powerlines come down in this one," he surmised.

"How do you want to handle the command post tonight?"

The Sheriff looked at the junior officer, but he did not answer immediately. Powell continued, "I'm willing to stand the first watch if you want to get on home to your family. I can almost imagine the worry you went through today."

"Thanks, Powell. I guess I will go on home, get some dry clothes and eat. It's really cold out there," he said as he shivered. "You call me if you hear anything; use the radio if the phones go out."

"Yes, Boss. I'll stay in your office or be down at dispatch if you want to reach me. Get some rest if you can."

"Yeah, I will, but I'll be back in four hours. Storm should be peaking at about then," the senior man reminded him.

"Yes, sir. I'll see you then," Powell spoke as he helped the Sheriff force open the door against the powerful wind. He called after Stone to drive carefully, but the words were lost and drowned in a noisy gust of stormy swirls.

After a couple of very busy hours at the police headquarters, the activity seemed to subside as most of the citizens were finally safe at home and in shelters. There was hardly any traffic to report, and all lights were operational. One ambulance was out on call to the country home of a near-term pregnant woman. Other than that emergency, the hospital was experiencing business as usual. The storm had deteriorated to a few gusts of wind in a steady downpour. The weatherman's report said that the storm was diminishing but issued flash-flood warnings.

Powell telephoned the Sheriff with the good news. They decided to disband the command post and bring in all but a few of the mobile units. Stone wanted hourly reports from the main bridges and updates on the river crests at all three rivers. Powell passed the order along through dispatch to notify the men. As he prepared to leave work and go home, he picked up the magazine he had gotten earlier in the day from the Chamber of Commerce.

It was not a very long drive to Powell's home from his office, but the road and visibility conditions made the going very slow. As he went into his kitchen, he grabbed a small towel and dried his hair before taking off his shirt. When he walked by the stove, he turned on the burner under the hot water kettle. He would get a warm sweatshirt and have a hot cup of instant coffee.

Something about the dash through the cold rain to his house had invigorated him. He prepared the coffee and sat down in his favorite chair to relax a little. He had the new magazine with him, and he decided to read awhile before going to bed. As he scanned the features listed on the front page, he was immediately drawn to the story of the criminal investigation of the infamous, Alferd Packer.

꒜

Alferd Packer was a young man in 1873 when he set out from Utah. He and the other members of the 21-man prospecting party were determined to make it to the rich mining fields of Colorado as soon as possible. As they wintered near the modern day city of Delta, Colorado, they dreamed of the treasures that awaited them in the San Juan Mountains. When the new year finally came, Packer was extremely anxious to leave the Ute Territory and press onward toward Central Colorado.

Packer and five companions decided in February of 1874 to brave the possibility of winter snowstorms and try to beat the other members of the party to the Los Piños Indian Agency just south of the cow-camp that would one day be called Gunnison. Taking only seven days worth of supplies with them, they headed for the unknown regions ahead.

By mid-April, nothing had been heard of the Packer group until one day Alferd Packer himself showed up at the agency. He claimed that his party had been snowed in and had run out of food. He said that because his feet were frozen, the others deserted him, leaving him to die alone in a blizzard. He later changed his story to say that he, being the best hunter in the group, had struck out on his own to try and secure game.

In any event, he was a few days later reunited with his companions only to find that all of them except Shannon Wilson Bell had been murdered. He swore that Bell had killed the other men and had even attacked him upon his return. In his defense, he claimed he had had no choice but to shoot Bell when Bell came after him with an axe.

Because of the many inconsistencies in his story, law officials decided to try and find the bodies of the missing men. They hoped that the crime scene would provide them with the proof that would either convict or acquit Packer. The lawmen were particularly appalled at what Packer had told them about the starvation conditions that had existed. Packer had said that they were so hungry that they had even boiled their own moccasins to eat. This had forced the men to bind up their feet with strips of blankets.

Alferd Packer agreed to lead a posse back to the area to try and find the bodies of his dead companions. Although he claimed that he was not exactly certain where the bodies were, he was able to lead the men to the general vicinity. After a widespread search, the dead men were found. The horror of their deaths was nothing compared to the revealing evidence that showed that the men had been cannibalized.

Packer then told a new story. He continued to insist that it was Bell that had killed and eaten the foursome, and that he had only killed Bell in self defense when the man attacked him to eat him. He claimed that Bell had gone insane from being trapped in the snow and starving to death. The local law enforcement did not believe his account, and he was arrested.

Alferd Packer was a clever man and managed to escape. He remained a fugitive at large for nine years. He was finally captured in Wyoming when one of the original members of the 21-man party spotted him. He was returned to Colorado to face sentencing under the new judicial system. Instead of being sentenced to hanging, he was given a forty-year sentence.

Throughout his incarceration, there were still people who believed his story and sought to help him prove his innocence. He completed 17 years in jail before receiving his parole. He died six years later leaving many questions still unanswered. Through the years, the matter of his cannibalism continued to be of interest to forensic departments. In the summer of 1989, the bodies of Packer's victims were exhumed from their graves at the base of Slumgullion Pass just a short distance from Lake City.

Anthropologists and other experts were invited to review the bodies. As the scientists studied the remains of the corpses, there was a consensus that the men had indeed been killed violently, probably by an axe. There was also supporting evidence that there had been cannibalism. What the experts could not tell, was who had actually done the killing. The mystery would remain regarding the truth or fiction of Packer's testimony.

✧∴∾

"Gruesome reading," Tim Powell said aloud to his quiet house. "Nothing like a grisly murder before bed time." He put the magazine down beside the empty coffee cup and headed down the hall toward his bedroom. He did not bother to turn off any lights as he listened to the howl of the wind outside the house.

14

Marva Lee Linden got up from her bed. Without turning on a light, she crossed the room to look out of the bedroom window. The window pane was so rained streaked that it took her several minutes before she could focus on the park across the way. She could see in the park's lamp light that the rain was still falling in torrential sheets. She stood several minutes watching the storm and listening to the raindrops pelting her house. In the far distance, there were flashes of light in the sky followed by deep, low rumblings.

During the brief moments that the lightning illuminated the night, Marva Lee caught sight of her own reflection in the window. She could see that her white hair framed her small face in a rather pleasant way. Her hair had a softness and a natural curl that had always made her proud, but she was more proud of her personal accomplishments. She had managed to make her own way through the world, fully independent and beholden to no one except God her maker.

Marva Lee felt the vibration of a close thunderclap and shivered in the shadows. Ever since she was a little girl, she had been fascinated by the power and majesty of storms. She hated the awful destruction they often caused, but she was awed by the enormity of their strength. Storms often reminded her of her dear father, the way they could sound so strong and yet be so gentle as to bring the much needed rain to the trees and flowers.

Her mind flashed to her garden, and she began to hope that the storm had not done too much damage. At one point during the evening, she had feared that she had heard hail. It had turned out not to be hail, however, only the wind-driven rain. She was thankful for small blessings. As soon as it was light, she planned to go out into the garden and check her flowers.

Now that she was getting older, Marva Lee had discovered that she needed far less sleep than she had needed as a young woman. She assumed that it was nature's way of helping her manage each of the remaining days of her so-called golden years. She recalled that her own grandmother had once told her to keep as busy as possible for there would be plenty of time to rest in the grave. Marva Lee doubted very much that she would rest in peace. It just would not be her style. She planned to be active forever.

The woman switched on the bedside lamp and sat down in the soft chair near her bed. For some reason that she could not explain, she felt uneasy. Marva Lee dismissed the storm as the reason for her unexplained anxiety and considered the possibility that her conversation with the Sheriff might have upset her more than she realized. Her mind kept going back to the pathetic Jasper Wilson and his overly painted wife.

As she took a deep breath, the secretary also recalled the ashen color of Judge Winfield's face as he hurried out of the office that afternoon. He had rushed passed her with a fearful, determined look that he always had when he was complaining about heartburn. He did not need to tell her that he was hurrying to a pharmacy for medicine; he had explained the symptoms to her several times before during the past couple of months.

She made a mental note to see if she could talk Winfield into seeing Dr. Kellog. It would not be that difficult to get an appointment, she surmised. A man of Winfield's age and condition might have something seriously wrong; and as much as she tried not to consider the possibility, she suspected that the former Judge might have a heart problem. He was definitely suffering from some malady.

The Judge's condition had seemed to worsen ever since the news of Big Jim Clancy's death. She could not help noticing that the Judge seemed to be brooding even more than usual since Sheriff Stone's visit to the office. Wrinkling her tiny nose as though she smelled something foul, Marva Lee puzzled over the mysterious relationship of the Judge and Clancy. With enough time, she determined, she would ferret out the secret. Her mind was made up.

She decided to read. Looking through the stack of recent magazines by her bedside, she found a new one. Glancing at it, the woman rejected it immediately stating under her breath, "I am certainly not going to read any more garbage about that fool, Packer! His momma didn't have enough sense to name him Alfred instead of Alferd. Hopeless!"

She tossed the magazine to the floor, and laughed aloud remembering a t-shirt she had seen the summer before. It had Packer's picture on it and said, "Have a Friend for Dinner."

.·.≀

Thunderstorms always bothered Jasper Wilson. He supposed it stemmed from his early days as a cattleman worrying about his herds. More than once, he had found that his terrified animals had grouped together along the barbed wire fences only to be electrocuted. In his mind, he could still hear their bawling in the night. He pictured their frightened eyes as they pushed their way into a large pack trying to find shelter from the awful noise of the thunder and the sting of the wind-driven rain. Hailstorms sometimes drove them to temporary madness.

Wilson knew about madness. His mother had suffered from it for years before his father had been forced to have her institutionalized. There had not been much to do or say about it back then, but he did recall that she had cried so much after his baby sister died that he did not think it was humanly possible to have that many tears. Consequently, he never cried. He did not want to end up like his mother; when she left their home, she did not even know who she was or what day it was. She would not talk to him or his father. Saying good-bye had been like talking to a cold, stone wall. There were no last hugs for the young boy.

Wilson had grown up thinking that women were the weaker sex, but his life with Yvonne was starting to convince him otherwise. He knew that he had been as generous and as kind to the young beauty as he could possibly be, but still she had never returned his love. He was not certain what it was that was missing in their relationship, but there had never been any true love for either of them.

Voni was a free spirit, and at first he had admired that in her. After the incident when she lost the baby, he had been so consumed by guilt that he thought he would never be able to make it up to her. He remembered the days so long ago when they were first married and lived at the ranch. He had been a fool to have

77

given her permission to ride the Arabian. It was far too spirited for her, and her fall had ended not only the pregnancy but any hope of future children.

He had taken his wife to the best clinic in Denver, but there had been no way for them to save the baby. The fall had simply caused too much damage to the young girl. For awhile after he heard the bad news, he did not even want to live. Eventually, he made a vow to himself that he would make it up to her and give her everything her heart could desire.

Throughout the passing years, he had been her faithful provider. He had indulged all of her endless whims and fancies. For years, he had looked the other way while she accumulated a mountain of gambling debts that he always made covert arrangements to repay. She had even borrowed from Clancy, he knew, but Clancy had refused to take any repayment from him claiming that he had plenty to share with his partner and a partner's wife. he told Wilson that they were the only real family that he had in the world.

Wilson was finished punishing himself. He was making changes in his relationship with his wife. No longer would he cover up for her debts. No longer would he drive a beat-up old car so that she could have a new vehicle every year. Jasper Wilson was a new man as far as he was concerned. He refused to be taken for a fool any longer.

Even in his anger, he had to admit to himself that there had been happy days in the past. He and Yvonne had enjoyed the country life for many months. He had continued to contribute to the local charities, giving this church group or that civic organization sides of beef for a barbecue fund raiser or whatever. He had been a prosperous man back then.

Later, Yvonne began to complain about feeling isolated and lonely out in the country with no one around to visit. He never had understood that logic, though, as she always seemed to be on the telephone or off to town until the stores closed. He did realize that there really was not anyone else her own age within miles of their place, and he was determined to please her.

Wilson sold a parcel of acreage to a developer, and with that money, he was able to afford a very nice house in Gunnison. They moved to town and had lived there ever since. Yvonne, he knew, had spent a fortune decorating and redecorating the place, but he did not complain as she seemed to be happier than ever before. That state of bliss remained until their last vacation trip to Las Vegas.

Voni had insisted that she wanted to go to Las Vegas and would not consider any other destination. Jasper recalled that he had wanted to take one of the annual fall foliage tours in New England, a place he had always dreamed of visiting, but his wife had been adamant on the subject. She had told him that if he could not or would not go along with her, she would go by herself. Rather than send her off alone, he consented to go.

In retrospect, he wished that he had not gone. He rarely saw his wife during the entire week that they were in Vegas. She stayed late in the casinos every night, then wanted to sleep-in each morning. He, on the other hand, was an early riser and preferred to be up with the sun and strolling the streets or swimming laps in the hotel's pool in the morning. During one of his early morning outings, he discovered a breakfast place that served a hearty meal for 99 cents.

Yvonne, in contrast, rose around noon when the bellboy arrived with room service. After a quick meal, she would go back down to the gaming tables and remain for most of the day. On occasion, she wandered over to the slot machines and played the one-armed bandits until she either ran out of change or had tired her arm. When it came to gambling, she was like a shark in a feeding frenzy. She could not seem to quit even when better judgment suggested otherwise.

Jasper had been thoroughly disgusted with her, though, when he found out later that she had even pawned her engagement ring to keep on playing the last day that they were there. He had believed that the ring meant something special to her, and he was more than disappointed when he found out otherwise. He could still recall his even greater shock when he discovered that his wife had retrieved the ring and was once again wearing it. At the time, she claimed that she had written to the pawn shop and redeemed the diamond; but he learned later that Big Jim had gone up there on business and had gotten it back for her.

Wilson did not confront her about the matter because in a naïve way, he believed that the ring had significance for her after all. It really did not occur to him that the big stone made for wonderful, instant collateral whenever she gambled. Since she had never let him see the claim ticket, he had no idea what it had cost Big Jim to secure the ring, but he felt a measure of gratitude for the efforts of his partner.

Now, he just wished that he had been more alert to the friendship that was developing between the big man and Voni. Maybe, he remorsed, he could have done something to head off the entanglement. Maybe, he criticized himself, he should have expected more from her and not spoiled her quite so much. What was done was done, he remembered sadly. There would be no going back in time to set things right.

~:~

Sheriff Stone looked in on his sleeping son for what seemed like the tenth time that night. Stone knew that he would never be more grateful than he was at that moment. Recalling the awful fear that had seized him when he first heard about the parks' crew injuries, he rubbed his hand across his mouth to stifle a little moan that threatened to escape. He had felt so helpless and so powerless, a feeling that he was not at all accustomed to experiencing.

Watching his son lying there so peacefully, Stone considered the sleep of the innocent. There was nothing like a clear conscience to aid the drowsy. He wondered, though if there was a certain guilty party out in the stormy night who was having troubled thoughts. Someone out there who might be having haunting nightmares about the murder of Big Jim Clancy.

~:~

Yvonne Wilson was restless. She could sense that her husband was downstairs moving around in the kitchen; although she could not actually hear him because of the noise the rain was making on the roof. She wondered what he was doing down there but was too tired to go down and have a look for herself. She knew her husband had been acting strangely for several weeks, but the death of his partner had seemed to make him more edgy than usual.

She reminded herself that she was glad that Jim Clancy was dead. He had always spelled trouble for her even though she had been attracted to him like a moth to a flame. Ever since her high school days, she had had a crush on Clancy, but the feeling had not been mutual. Clancy had used her and then dumped her for someone else. She had been so angry at the time that she had vowed that someday she would get even with him. Opportunity presented itself when she discovered that she was pregnant.

Rather than tell Clancy that she was carrying his child, she opted to pretend that she did not know who the father was. When her parents suggested that Jasper Wilson was willing to be her husband, Yvonne jumped at the chance. Hoping to put Clancy in his place by letting him see that another man found her desirable and was willing to marry her, she agreed to the matrimony. She was certain that Clancy would regret the day he rejected her, especially when he saw the baby that would look just like him! What she had not counted on was the kindness and the generosity of Jasper Wilson.

Jasper's love for her had softened her heart as well as her anger. She did not want to bring into the world a child who had any relationship to Jim Clancy. In fact, she recalled in horror, the many nightmares she had experienced when her dreams showed the newborn baby to be the image of his real father.

When she was in high school, she heard stories about women who had miscarriages after a fall. Rather than take a chance that her unborn baby be born looking just like his father and cause embarrassment for both her and Jasper, she decided to abort the child. The only way she could think of to do it was a fall. That's when she got the idea to talk Jasper into letting her ride the new Arabian. She did not count on the terrible pain nor the possible sterility when she turned loosed of the reins and tumbled to the ground.

That all seemed so very long ago. Over the years, her attitude toward Clancy had changed, and she learned to accept him the way he was. She even told herself that the reason the big man had never married was because he had never found another woman who could measure up to her. In the last few months, things were different. Clancy had become very demanding, insisting on payment of debts that he had before forgiven. He no longer desired her company, he told her. She was made to feel like a silly school girl all over again...She hated him!

15

Sheriff Stone was very unhappy when he got to work that morning and found the roof over his office had leaked. His secretary had strategically placed a bucket and a couple of flowerpots to catch the errant drips, but the carpet was so soggy, he could hear his footsteps on the wet fabric.

"What a mess!" he groaned. "Tell me this isn't Friday the 13th."

Deputy Powell arrived in time to respond to the comment, "It's Friday all right, Boss, but it is definitely not the thirteenth."

The secretary merely shook her head and replaced a water-filled wastebasket with an empty one.

"Sir, I was going to suggest that you move your stuff to my office," the junior officer recommended. "The way the wind blew the rain, it's only this end of the hall that caught it."

"Thanks, Powell. I may take you up on that, at least until maintenance can get in here with the Wet-Vac. Otherwise, I don't think I'm going to get much done," he spoke with disappointment in his voice. "Last night was probably the biggest storm that we've had since we moved into this building. Guess we shouldn't have expected to get off scot-free. We're in good shape compared to a couple of places in town."

"That's right. Reports are in that a tree caved in a garage over on Bidwell. Nobody hurt, but quite a bit of damage to the car and such," Powell informed him.

"Bidwell? By the rodeo grounds?" the Sheriff inquired.

"Yes, sir. A block or so west of there."

"Any other major damage in town?" the officer wanted to know.

"Golf course has a lot of limbs down, no damage to any of the major buildings. There was the regular crop of washouts along the

Gunnison River. Heard one man was filing a complaint against the city because water got up in his tool shed. He was served papers last year for building too close to the river's edge. I can't imagine how he thinks he has a leg to stand on," Powell concluded.

"I understand that one of our units got in some chain saw practice last night. Dispatch notified me around midnight that the boys took care of a big tree partially blocking the road to the nursing home."

"Yes, sir. Someone at the nursing home called it in. When the men were finished and getting ready to leave, a couple of the old gentlemen insisted that they go inside to dry off and warm up. There was hot chocolate and sandwiches waiting for them as well as some big dry towels. I can tell you they really appreciated the hospitality at that time of night."

"That's great. We are here to serve. Don't ever forget that."

"No, sir," the younger man replied.

"Let's see if in all of the chaos, we can find the status of the APB on the missing Bronco. Also put in a call to Grand Junction about Ben Peek's condition. Ask the officers in charge to quiz Peek and find out where Hayden is likely to have gone."

"Right away. Anything else?"

"Yeah, as a matter of fact, phone the Lake City law and find out if any of Clancy's property has shown up down there. If not, advise them to be on the look-out at the flea market tomorrow morning."

"Will do. I'll get on this right now." Powell hurried out of the office as quickly as he could. He was afraid that if he lingered, the Sheriff would continue adding items to the checklist. Powell knew that he had enough work to do to keep himself busy for three days, let alone one.

Sheriff Stone watched the young man rush down the hall, and then he remembered that there was one other item he wanted to have the young man take care of. He telephoned the Courthouse and requested a search warrant and a permit for a hair sample.

༺ ༻

Because of the higher altitude and surrounding peaks, Crested Butte had been spared the brunt of the storm. Tourists were already starting to filter into the village in anticipation of the two-week long

Balloon Festival. The fact that there was always plenty of activities in Crested Butte made the little town, popular year-round. It seemed to the locals that they rarely had a break from the influx of crowds.

As an authentic 100-year-old mining town. Crested Butte flaunted its past and its Victorian styles. It could boast a dozen activities throughout the year, no matter what the season. From the early spring, a carpet of wildflowers appeared to captivate the photographer as well as the hiker. Chairlift rides up Mt. Crested Butte provided a bird's eye view of the fields of pastel columbines, tall and stately larkspur that would give way to blankets of daisies and crimson paintbrushes.

As the snow run-off increased, rafters would take to the waters around Crested Butte. Upstream, the quiet Slate River would become a torrent of rushing rapids and dangerous waterfalls to be tackled only by the hardiest sportsmen. With sections along the stream named "Wicked Wanda" and "Dead Man's Curve," the Slate provided a never-to-be-forgotten ride.

The more sedentary crowd could choose to limit the river time to fishing, either from the shores or in chest-high waders in the middle of the icy shallows. Where the rowdy rivers were under control, the fisherman lined the banks waiting for the rainbow trout; while solitary men spent time and effort selecting the perfect fly or the perfect bait for the time and place. Gold medal fishing was everywhere.

⌣⁚∾

Kate Mason was very glad that she had made the move from Vail. Although she missed the Bavarian-style architecture of the other resort, and the glamorous atmosphere, there were too many unhappy memories for her in the Vail area. She did miss the students that she had taught and often wondered what had become of them. Several students had sent her get well cards when she first left her position. She imagined that most of them had forgotten her by now. Which was as it should be, she decided. Life had to go on for everyone.

Kate Mason felt fortunate to be as well situated and as well received in the community as she was. She realized that it would not be easy for a small village to accept a newcomer as a permanent part of the establishment. She made every effort to comply with what she perceived to be the standards of the little town, and she had tried desperately to have her business blend in with the rest of the shops and their offerings. She had even agreed to sponsor one of the town's softball teams, although she knew practically nothing about the sport. Kate wanted to be treated as an integral part of the community life.

Life, the word hurt her just to think it. Four tiny letters, she considered, that meant so much. She could not and would not complain about her lot in life, she decided. There was not enough time to relive the past or worry about the future. She only wished that she had been that philosophical sooner.

⋰⋱

At Gothic, Jeff Harper looked out of his laboratory window at the beautiful day ahead. It was one of those superbly lovely ones that made the Rocky Mountains famous in summer. He doubted that at that moment there could be any place lovelier on earth. He smiled to himself to think that Gothic might have been the original Garden of Eden, except for the fact that the surrounding area was always the coldest spot in the nation throughout the fall and winter. He did not believe that God would have wanted Adam and Eve traipsing around in the frozen powder.

He decided to telephone Kate and ask her to meet him for a tennis game at four. It was a day too lovely to waste.

16

Willis Miller thought about shaving, then decided against it. In his one-room efficiency, he had all the comforts he needed, and shaving just to look good for the public did not seem to matter at his age and station in life. He felt well and looked forward to spending the day with his friends.

Willis knew that the local townsfolk could not see nor hear his departed comrades, but that did not make them any less real to him. He knew things that other people did not know for he had looked Death itself in the face years ago in the war. What he saw was a terrible sight that was horrifying enough to turn any man away from mischief and put him on the straight and narrow path. He wished that path were not quite so straight and quite so narrow as he believed he sometimes needed the help of a good drink to ease the pain in his missing arm.

The doctors told him years ago that he would experience what they called "phantom pain." They did not tell him that he would be able to endure it; they only offered mild prescription medications that had long since ceased to be effective. He frequently went back to the VA Hospital to increase the dosage, but it still had not helped. The doctors in charge of his case told him that short of drugs that would incapacitate him, the only thing left was to suffer through to the end.

He suffered plenty, he acknowledged. The pain seldom let up for more than an hour or two at a time, but somehow, when he was talking to his fallen comrades, he was distracted enough to forget the hurt. He regretted that the others in Gunnison could not communicate with his friends. He knew what fine men they were when they lived. Why, he was just telling Ed Campbell the other day what a good soldier he had been.

It was Ed Campbell from West Virginia who inspired him that morning near the German border. Ed was always being teased by the other men about his Scottish heritage, especially when it was his turn to pick up the tab. Anyway, that last morning when they were all dead tired from trying to keep up with General Patton, Ed had put on a brief but inspiring show.

Hiking his trousers up to his thigh, he wrapped a towel around him like a kilt and proceeded to dance a Highland Fling for the men. He hummed a tune and danced with fury as he hopped and jumped. Twirling and pointing his toe with his heavy boot, he was a sight to behold. Instead of a sword, he danced over his rifle; and except for the pauses when he had to stop and retie his towel, he was a laughing, humming inspiration for war-weary men. For a brief time, he ceased to be a corporal in the Army and became a link with the civilized world in a better time.

After a few minutes, several of the other men joined in trying to imitate what they saw, but the booming voice of the Sergeant soon put the fun to rest as he called out the chow line. Everybody scrambled to the latrines and to the mess tent except Ed Campbell and one or two others who lay in a laughing, exhausted heap on the frozen ground.

Willis Miller could still remember that morning as if it were yesterday. In fact, the entire day was etched in his mind forever as the battle in the afternoon would claim the lives of the men he had trained with and fought beside. As far as he knew, he was the only survivor. He was wounded so severely, that after being unconscious for more than a week, for a period of time he could recall nothing. The surgeons told him that the amputation and the concussion combined to traumatize his system in such a way that he might never have a good memory recall after the incident. Yet, the actual day of the battle remained crystal clear up to the point when the shell had exploded near them.

During his lengthy convalescence, he tried to find out the fate of his friends. Every agency he contacted replied the they had all been killed on that same day. One organization years later told him that they were all buried in the American Cemetary outside of the Luxembourg capital. They were at rest in the same manicured grounds as their beloved leader, General George Patton.

Miller wrote to the U.S. agency in charge of the Memorial

Park and inquired about his comrades. In return, they sent him a complete list of names of those who were buried there. He searched the list, checking off the names of four of his pals, but he never found Ed Campbell's name. He did note that there was a considerable number of plots labeled, "unknown soldier." For a time after reading the names and weeping at the memories, he felt a tremendous sense of guilt that he had not died with the others. He figured God had him on another timetable. He did not know why he was spared, but there must have been a good reason, he reckoned.

Except for his hitch in the Army, Willis Miller had lived all of his life in and around Gunnison. He was a well-known figure who mostly kept to himself. he lived quite comfortably on his pension and the dividends from some investments and stocks that he had purchased before the war. Some people thought that if the truth be known, Willis Miller was a wealthy man. There was speculation that his family had bequeathed him a handsome amount, mostly in the form of shares of IBM.

Everyone in town agreed on one thing, Willis Miller was not much to look at. His baggy clothes were from the second hand store, and he always looked as though he needed a shave. He did keep his hair trimmed by the local barber, and in the early years after the war, several of the local ladies made offers to help take care of him. It was a nuisance though to try and compete in a conversation with the voices that haunted the man.

After a few years, people in town stopped trying to talk to the veteran. They gave and returned polite nods and smiles, but that was about the extent of his contact with the people, except for Miss Marva Lee Linden who was always wanting to hire him to fix one thing or another on the big house she owned. He did not need her money, but he took the jobs because he liked her chatty ways. In the summer, she always gave him flowers and vegetables from her garden as well as cash for a job. He enjoyed the work, for it was always some small thing to take care of that he could manage easily with one arm. As a token of friendship, he frequently left a trout, wrapped in newspaper, on her back step.

As he thought about the trout for Miss Linden, he considered returning to the Roaring Judy. He wanted to go back and see Sheriff Stone again. He liked the County Sheriff. He wanted to see the lawman and tell him about something he remembered after they last spoke, but for the time being, he could not recall what it was that he needed to remember. "Maybe," he reminded himself aloud, "Ed or one of the boys can jog my memory!"

∴

At the Police Headquarters, Sheriff Stone was finally free to return to his office. The leaks had been fixed by the roofing crew, and the carpet was dried as much as possible. Big fans were set up around the room to blow warm dry air into the area to help get rid of the excessive moisture. The fans were noisy though, and his secretary was forever running after pages that blew off of her desk.

Powell returned to speak with the Sheriff, "Got those updates you wanted, Boss." He began to summarize what he found out about the tasks the senior officer had assigned him.

"First of all, Peek's doing real well. He should be released in a day or two. The local law will see to it that he gets put on a bus back here as soon as he is well enough to travel."

"Good. Did Peek say anything about Buck Hayden?" Stone asked.

"Yes, sir. he must have been feeling in a helpful mood, or else he was just being spiteful and nasty, but he did say that Hayden would probably head for Mexico or California."

"That's not a lot of help, Powell. We're talking a major amount of territory," he scowled as he spoke.

"True enough, but that's all we've got to go on. The law in Grand Junction thinks that Peek does not really have the answer. That's the best that they could do. On the bright side, we don't have to look toward the north or the east," the younger man tried to lighten the gloomy situation.

"What else have you got?" the Sheriff sounded tired.

"Well, it goes along with what Peek said. The APB has not turned up anything yet. Several states are actively looking for that Bronco," he reported.

"We're going to get that guy," Stone spoke with determination.

"We do have some good leads on the stolen merchandise. Lake City Police had a man turn in Clancy's television. The man claimed that he did not see the security engraving on the set until he got home. He has also told them that he saw some other items that might belong to Clancy. He described one of those large silver and turquoise wrist watch bands. Said there were the initials 'J. W. C.'

89

on the inside. The man selling the silver was asking too much for a flea market clientele, so he probably still has that piece."

"Now that's good. Any chance that the man was able to give a description of the seller to the police?"

"Yes, sir. Definitely sounds like Buck Hayden."

⌣∵⌣

Buck Hayden was enjoying himself in Red River, New Mexico. He had crossed the Colorado border a few days before after spending time in the Alamosa area. He decided that the Bronco with the New Mexico plates would be less conspicuous in its home state. Most of the time, he managed to park the truck in such a way that the front plate showed instead of the numbered tag. He knew it was a cat-and-mouse game with the law. In the meantime, he intended to lay low in Red River and mingle with the summer tourists. He could easily manage a trip or two to Taos if he got bored.

He looked down at the fancy silver and turquoise wrist watch and remembered the way that the waitress in the restaurant the night before had cooed over the timepiece. It was a work of art, and it made him feel good just to wear it. He felt he had been poor too long and that it was time for him to start enjoying life. After all, he reminded himself, he had made a killing at the flea market and had been able to unload nearly every item that he had taken from Clancy's cabin. With the paycheck that he had cashed down the street the day before, he had plenty of money to last him for weeks.

Since it was Friday, he intended to go over to the Community Center later and watch the square dancing festivities. He knew that Red River was one of the major towns to sponsor square dancing contests in the West, and he planned to be there early to watch the ladies in their short petticoats. He considered that he might even take a turn on the dance floor himself during the open dance time if he could find a willing partner.

There were things to do, he reminded himself. He needed to shine his boots and lay out one of his new shirts. He also planned to shower and try out his new cologne. As his hand touched his chin, he looked up at the mirror above the dresser and flinched from the sign of his own acne-scarred skin. It would take a heap of money and cologne, he reckoned, if a face like his were going to attract anyone to want to dance with him. Then he smiled, remembering the reaction of the lady looking at his expensive watch. Money, he thought, could be the root of all evil, but right then, he was more interested in the pleasure it might bring.

Before he started preparing for the dance, he looked out of the motel window to see that his Bronco was all right. he had backed the vehicle in to the parking place, and the tag was obscured by the shrubs that lined the walkway in front of the registration office. It looked for all the world to see as if it had been put there to facilitate the loading or unloading of luggage. However, Buck did not have much luggage when he arrived, only a wallet stuffed with cash and a paper bag or two of items he accumulated in Alamosa. When he got the Bronco, he was pleased to discover that it was very well supplied including a cache of bills hidden under the floor mat on the passenger's side.

He laughed a laugh that was more of a snort than anything. "When are they going to learn?" he questioned aloud in the empty room. "They shouldn't leave home without it!"

᷍᷍

Sheriff Stone told Deputy Powell that they needed to pick up a search warrant and head for Crested Butte after lunch.

The younger man went to finish up a few matters in his own office, then returned to join the Sheriff. Within a short time, the two men were on their way to the Courthouse, then on the road to Crested Butte.

As they drove along Highway 135, they spotted Willis Miller's old pickup truck pulled off of the road and onto the shoulder. They slowed down to see if there was any sign of the man near his vehicle, but continued onward when they saw that a small step stool was placed by the barbed wire fence along the road. It was obvious at once to both lawmen that Miller had used the stool to cross the fence of the posted "No Trespassing" field. From that point, it was an easy stroll down hill to the banks of the East River.

"Looks like Miller's hot after the fish today," the Deputy remarked.

"I forgot to tell you that I let the ranger know he could reopen the fishing park today. I think we've got all of the information from the scene that we are going to get. If Miller had checked with the ranger, he would not have had to go scampering over the wire."

"He's quite a guy," the young lawman offered.

"Yep, if he's still there when we come back by, maybe we can go down and have a talk with him. He may be our only witness as to what actually happened last week."

"Do you seriously think that his testimony on anything would hold water in a court of law?" Powell asked.

"Hopefully, it won't come to that. I am betting that when we get enough evidence, we will know who the murderer is beyond a shadow of doubt. It will only remain for that person to admit his or her guilt."

"You are still thinking that it could have been a woman that shot Clancy, Boss?"

"You bet, Powell. We have at least two female suspects that have registered .22s. The motives are still hazy, but they each had ample opportunity," he affirmed.

17

Sheriff Stone and Deputy Powell arrived in Crested Butte and drove straight to Kate Mason's shop at the end of Elk Avenue. It was always with a bit of apprehension, the lawmen remained constantly alert whenever serving a warrant. They had both been trained well enough in police procedures to fully realize that even the mildest appearing character could change into a deadly foe when cornered. Official documents produced a great deal of fear in the guilty as well as anxiety in the innocent. They knew that fact and proceeded accordingly. They did not want to frighten the woman, but they were well aware of the fact that she owned a gun. Calmly, they got out of the jeep and walked up the steps in front of the little store.

Kate Mason saw them as soon as they opened the door. She could tell right away by the serious look on Stone's face that the men were there on official business and not there to shop. For quite some time she had expected a visit from them. Now, as far as she was concerned, it would be a matter of how much to tell them and how much to keep to herself. They obviously were prepared to do something official, she noted, as the County Sheriff took out a folded paper from inside of his jacket.

Looking around the room and seeing that there were not customers present, Stone said, "Afternoon, Ms. Mason. I have some papers to serve you, and I think it would be best if you would close up the store until we are finished talking."

"Why certainly, Sheriff Stone," she agreed, trying to sound as cheerful and cooperative as she could. She crossed the showroom and locked the front door. She also turned the "Open" sign around.

"What seems to be the problem, Sheriff?" she asked warily.

"Ma'am, Deputy Powell and I have a search warrant issued in Gunnison giving us permission to search the premises and your automobile."

"Search? Search for what, gentlemen?" she feigned a tone of uncertainty.

"Yes, ma'am. We are investigating the murder of James W. Clancy, and we have reason to believe that you might own a handgun of the caliber used in his slaying. We know from a note written by Clancy that you were to see him last Friday, the day he died."

She caught her breath a bit, and both men heard the sound. "Oh, my word! Does that mean you are here to arrest me for Clancy's murder?" She looked visibly shaken.

"No, ma'am. We would just like for you to turn your gun over to us. We want to have Ballistics check it at the laboratory. We are also here to get a shoe print from a sampling of at least three pairs of your shoes."

"My shoes? But I don't see?" she asked, and then she remembered the mud that had been by the river that day.

"One other request, ma'am," Powell mentioned. "We need a hair sample. One from your hairbrush will do if you'll just show me where it is." The young man smiled at the woman and wanted to relieve her obvious discomfort.

"Yes. Yes, of course. Right this way." Kate led them to her upstairs apartment. She pointed out the small bathroom with its vanity cabinet for Powell to put a strand or two of hair in a plastic container he carried. Next, she opened the bifold doors of her wardrobe closet where she kept her shoes neatly arranged in a row in the back on the floor. Powell drew outlines on the cardboard models that the Investigation Room had given him.

While Powell was busy tracing the footprints, he noted that every pair of shoes was a size six. One pair in particular had the type of low, narrow heel that matched the impression taken at the scene. He told her that he would have to take that pair along with him back to the headquarters. They would be able to run a test on any mud particles that might remain on the well-cleaned shoes. There was always a chance that the forensic experts would pick up something the human eye could not detect.

In a way, Sheriff Stone felt sorry for the attractive woman. She really looked vulnerable and tiny standing there watching the officer work by her closet. In a way, he thought, they were violating her privacy, but it was necessary. Someone had murdered Clancy, and it could very well have been her.

When the younger officer was finished, Stone turned to her and said, "Now, if you will surrender the .22, we will be going along."

"I'm afraid I can't do that, officers," she spoke quietly.

Powell looked around the apartment wondering if they would be forced to "toss" the entire place to get the weapon.

Kate explained further, "After I heard about Big Jim's murder, I realized just how much I really do hate guns. I threw the thing in the trash that weekend. It's probably at the landfill by now."

Sheriff Stone and Powell looked at other. Both men were silent as they mentally reviewed their options. They could believe that Kate Mason was telling the truth, or they could tear the place apart on the off chance that she was lying. Either way, the prospects did not appear to be very good.

Kate broke the silence. "I assure you, Sheriff Stone. I really did get rid of the gun. Every time I thought about Jim...well, it made me shudder. Of course I had no way of knowing that you would come here looking for the gun," her voice shook somewhat and both men looked directly at her.

"Ma'am, I think you better sit down. You are looking a little pale," Powell offered and Stone nodded in agreement. They followed the lady out of the bedroom and into the small sitting room at the front of the house. From the bright sunny windows they could look out on the busy avenue and the mountains beyond.

Stone began, "You'll have to forgive us, ma'am, but this is a murder investigation, and we are just trying to do our duty. I want to believe you that the gun's not here, but I have an obligation to make a search. You understand, don't you?"

"Of course, Sheriff. I'm just sorry to have to take up your time like this," she replied.

"Powell, go back to the bedroom and give it a light once-over," the senior officer ordered.

"Yes, sir," the deputy replied, then left the room.

"Ms. Mason, is there anything at all you'd like to tell me about last Friday or your relationship with Jim Clancy? I assure you that what you tell me will be held in the strictest of confidence. I realize that you are a widow and want to maintain your good reputation, but if there is anything at all that you could tell me that would shed some light on what happened to Clancy, I would certainly appreciate it."

"I don't know quite how to begin. You already know that I am single. I did have a couple of dates with Clancy, but they were not what you would label romantic. He was interested in the Mountain Theater group, and so was I. We met at a fund raiser several weeks ago.

"Of course, I knew right away who he was because he had been so accurately described to me by my friend, Jeff Harper. There was no missing Big Jim when he was in a room. I rather think he liked being the center of attention. He had a sort of charisma that was almost irresistible. He definitely knew how to be charming when he wanted to be."

"Were you supposed to see him last Friday?" Stone asked.

"Yes, I was. We planned to go to a concert in Gunnison later that evening. I realized that I would not be able to attend, and tried to contact him. I phoned his cottage, but got no answer. I called the Kebler Pass Project office, and the man who answered told me that Jim usually fished at the Roaring Judy before going home. It did not seem to me to be too far away, so I drove out there to see if I could find him."

"Did you?" the Sheriff asked.

"Sheriff Stone," the woman replied hesitantly. "I really do not want to be involved in this."

"I'm afraid it's too late for that, Ms. Mason. You might as well tell me what you know."

"OK...when I arrived at the Roaring Judy, there were several cars already out there. I did see Jim's 4-Runner, so I knew he was somewhere around. There was an older man nearby loading his gear into an old pickup truck. I asked him if he knew Big Jim and if he had seen him. He directed me toward the river bank beyond the ponds.

{The weeds were as tall as I was, and I could not see a thing until I reached a clearing at the water's edge."

"Go on," Stone encouraged her.

"Oh, Sheriff, I am so ashamed," she stopped talking and started crying softly.

He waited for her to compose herself. He needed to hear the rest of her account. Finally, she was able to continue.

"You are going to think I am a coward and a terrible citizen when I tell you what happened next."

"Let me be the judge of that," he instructed her.

"I saw Jim lying there on the rocks. My first thought was that he was drunk and had passed out, but as I watched him for a moment, I saw he was lying too still. Suddenly, I felt very afraid. I hurried toward him, and then I saw the blood all over his shirt. I remember that I knelt down beside him and felt his neck to see if there was any pulse. There wasn't." The woman stopped talking waiting for the Sheriff to ask her the inevitable question.

"Why didn't you try and get help?" Stone asked in a tone harsher than he intended.

"I was frightened. I didn't know if the killer was still lurking around the area. All kinds of things went through my head. I knew Big Jim was always into all kinds of deals; and for all I knew, one of those deals might have gone sour. He was dead, and I might be next!" She almost sounded convincing.

"Did you see anyone else in the area? Anyone who might substantiate your story?" Stone questioned.

"No, I don't think so. The little man with the pickup was the only one I spoke to."

"Could you identify him if you saw him again?" the Sheriff had a good idea who she saw.

"Quite possible if he lives anywhere around here. He was the only man I have seen in the county with only one arm." She told him confirming his guess.

"Getting back to the gun, ma'am. Do you happen to recall what day you threw it out?"

"Monday, I think it was. Yes, I'm pretty sure it was Monday. That's our regular pick up day for the alley."

After a few more questions and even fewer answers, Stone called to Powell to desist in the search. It was time for them to leave. As they drove away, neither of them spoke for several minutes. Finally, Stone told his partner, "I hate to tell you where we are going next."

"I think I know, Boss. We're going out to talk to Charlie at the landfill, am I right?"

"Powell, I swear, you are getting smarter everyday," the older man congratulated the younger one. "Just hold your nose or you'll get a big whiff of the dump. It's just around the bend."

Kate Mason hurried to her bathroom and took two of the pills her doctor had given her. She was surprised to see how her hands were shaking as she fumbled with the cap on the medication. She knew that she could not afford to let herself get so upset. To be calm was what she needed. Her health could not afford to have any setbacks, or all the medicine in the world would not help her.

Thinking back on her interview with the Sheriff, she wished that she could have told him the whole truth. It probably would have made his job a lot easier, she surmised, but Kate did not believe that it was her personal obligation to give him all of the facts. He would find out the truth soon enough, she figured. Stone struck her as the kind of lawman that always gets his man, or his woman as the case might be, she mused.

Kate knew the officer was going to have his work cut out for him if he were going to solve the Clancy murder. There were just too many people in the county who were glad to be rid of Big Jim. She thought that was somewhat sad, and she almost pitied the man. Then, she remembered what he had done to her.

∴

Stone and Powell were greeted at the landfill by Charlie. Charlie had been in charge of the site for as long as anyone could remember. He seemed to be the only permanent employee on the city rolls. No one else wanted his job, and the village of Crested Butte was happy to retain his services for as long as possible.

The Sheriff explained to Charlie that they were looking for a gun that might have been disposed of on or about Monday behind Elk Avenue. Charlie told them that he had not come across the weapon, but there was a metal detector he could use if they wanted him to try. The Sheriff agreed that it would help them a lot if he could find the pistol. Charlie said that he would start looking in his spare time and would phone the Sheriff if anything turned up.

Sheriff Stone took a twenty dollar bill out of his wallet and insisted that Charlie take it "for his time." Finding the weapon was a priority as far as Stone was concerned, although he still was not convinced of the validity of the Mason woman's story. Something about it was not right, as far as he was concerned. He knew it was highly probable that she had not disposed of the gun, but if Charlie was willing to search for it, he could at least hope the handgun would be found.

18

It was almost four o'clock when Kate Mason left her house to join Jeff Harper. The weather was perfect as she drove through the village and up the steep road that led to Mt. Crested Butte. The flowers along the roadway were so thick ad luxuriant in places that they actually encroached onto the pavement beside her car. Both sides of the incline road were covered with bouquets of black-eyed Susans and daisies. Purple-blue daisies, with their pink and white cousins sought supremacy in splendor along the route.

Driving past the hotels and condominiums, she was soon in the residential area. Within ten minutes, she reached the City Park on Gothic Road. As she removed her tennis gear from the car, she looked across the wide valley. She could see the stables just beyond the City Services Center, but there was no sign of Jeff Harper. She wondered if he would be delayed for long.

She welcomed the chance to have a few moments alone in the beautiful setting. Ever since the Sheriff and his Deputy left her apartment, she felt the need to get away, to get some fresh air. It went against her conscience to be so uncooperative with the lawmen, but she reminded herself that she had her reasons. She also hoped, though, that she was not just being vindictive. The trouble and lack of cooperation she had had with the police in Vail had destroyed her faith in the so-called "system."

She sat down on the steps that led to the tennis courts and admired the natural beauty of the surroundings. As far as the eye could see, there were tall, tree-covered mountains towering in the distance. Wooded hills sloped toward the open meadow of the stables, and a deep gulch, softened with a riot of colorful flowers, marked the boundary line of the park.

Giant ship-sized clouds sailed majestically overhead as though they had a timetable to keep. They rushed across the sky, while wisps of a lighter mist trailed lazily below. A partial rainbow peaked from behind one of the billowing structures as if to alert the watchful. The clouds' enormous shadows crossed the land creating a variety of patterns of light along the way.

Watching the clouds and listening to the quiet hum of the honeybees in the wildflowers, Kate was suddenly aware of the sound of children's laughter. She looked up to see two children playing a game of tag as they headed for the playground equipment. A minute later, a young woman joined the children, and Kate assumed that she was their mother.

A tear spilled over her cheek as she remembered her own daughter:

Sunny Lynn Mason had been the most wonderful child. She had been as cheerful and bright in looks and personality as her name implied. Since her earliest childhood, she had been a joy to her parents. A warm and loving girl, she grew more intelligent and beautiful with each birthday.

As a teenager, she began to reach her maturity. Not only was she fair of face and hair, but everywhere she went, people were impressed by her various musical talents and her ability to communicate. Her company was sought by girls as well as by her many male admirers. She was a disarmingly charming tomboy who willingly participated in almost every sport. Early on, her mother had warned her that boys would be discouraged by a girl who always won every competition, but in the end, the mother had been wrong. Sunny always played fair, and her enthusiasm showed in everything she attempted. She simply wanted to be the best.

Being the best had proved to present a conflict between her and her mother as the young girl finished high school. Her mother wanted her to remain in the Denver area and attend college, but Sunny had other plans. She applied to and was accepted by the University of Kansas. The scholarship they offered her more than paid for her education. She was determined to go to school in Lawrence.

There were tears and anger for several weeks, but both women knew that in the end, it was the girl who would have to make the decision. Her mother felt rejected by her choice to move from home, but for Sunny it was merely a chance to grow and learn. She believed she needed the independence she could get only by living away from home. After so many years of caring and sharing with her widowed mother, she knew she needed to be free to chart new horizons for herself.

Kate had taken the youngster's decision very badly. She had tried to make her daughter feel guilty about deserting her. Day after day, they argued about the expense, the distance, and the loneliness that each would experience. In the end, Kate had to reluctantly agree that her daughter would have to do what she believed to be right, but it was just the beginning of the great emptiness.

Time proved that Sunny was correct. She had a wonderfully successful four years at the university, winning all kinds of honors and making many new friends. Her mother even learned to adjust to seeing her only during the holiday breaks and keeping in touch by mail and by telephone. Sunny finished her degree, and informed her mother that she would return to Colorado.

The girl's mother hoped that Sunny would be able to live with her in Denver once again, but it was not to be. She received a position as a teaching assistant at the University of Colorado in Boulder. There, she would continue her studies for a Master of Science Degree in her chosen field of chemistry. She informed her mother that the grant and the work-study program were too valuable to refuse. They would be able to see each other most weekends.

At first, the arrangement was pleasant, but as the school work progressed and became more difficult, Sunny found that she needed to remain on the campus and in the lab more hours. As the winter weather set in, the girl was spending most of her waking hours on her research. It was in the lab that she met her future husband, the young scientist, Joseph Martell.

From the moment she met him, Kate liked her future son-in-law. He was as charming and articulate as he was handsome. She could immediately see why her daughter was attracted to him. The engagement ring he chose for Sunny was one of the most beautiful and original designs that she had ever seen. Their future together looked very bright, and they made plans for a Christmas wedding. They agreed that that was the only time they would both be free enough from their work to schedule a brief honeymoon.

The wedding was small but elegant. The little church they attended in Denver was decorated with unadorned Christmas trees, and what seemed like miles of wide, white satin ribbon linking giant bow after giant bow at each pew. Each bow framed a cluster of large white gardenias tucked with tiny pink tea roses. Tall white candles and more white and pink flowers surrounded the altar. The fragrance was a wonderful combination of the natural perfumes.

Sunny looked like an angel in her beautiful gown. As her good friend and favorite professor escorted her down the aisle, her mother looked on at the beautiful young woman her daughter had become. All lace and filmy organza, Sunny emerged from her veil to be kissed by her groom.

The reception was a simple affair held in the church's activities room. After cutting the cake, the couple disappeared briefly to prepare for their journey. A few minutes later, they returned to do the traditional honors of throwing the garter and the bride's bouquet. The guests then showered them with rice as they prepared to leave on their wedding trip to Vail.

It was snowing by the time the happy couple arrived in the quaint resort of Vail, Colorado. They turned off of Interstate 70 and drove toward the village proper. In spite of the increasing snow, they could see the ski lifts and the carefree skiers. Twilight was settling fast, but the white of the landscape made it seem not as dark as it might for that time of year.

As they neared their hotel, they stopped at a stop sign before preparing to make a right hand turn into the parking lot. They never made the turn. A drunk driver came from behind and slammed into them at high speed. They never heard nor saw another thing before their young lives were taken.

Kate could remember Sunny and rejoiced for the happy time she had with her. She wanted to forgive the driver that had taken her daughter's life, but she doubted that it would ever be possible. She had been so angry at the time of the accident. She had grieved, and she had screamed. For a while, she denied that the accident had even occurred. Little by little, she forced herself to spend time coaxing the police and her attorney to take action against the driver. She soon learned that the wealthy man who had killed her daughter had been released on bail and had returned to his own hometown in another part of the state. Kate had not met the man at the time, but she knew his name and address.

Kate herself began to suffer from physical pains and sought medical help within a few weeks after the accident, for she knew that it was not unusual for a bereaved person to become ill following the death of a loved one. What she did not know was that her illness was such that the doctor did not give her long to live. At that point, it really did not matter to her. As far as she was concerned, her life was over anyway. Her daughter was all the family she had in the world. Then, terrible thoughts of revenge began to fill her mind.

Suddenly, she had a reason to live. Her condition went into remission and her health improved. She was determined to bring the guilty man to justice even if she had to exact the justice herself. She purchased a handgun and ammunition before she moved to Gunnison County. Her plans began to crystalize as she carefully stalked her prey.

"Kate!" Harper called out, momentarily startling her. "Sorry I'm late. Got a last minute phone call from D.C."

"Quite all right," she told him happily. "I was just enjoying the day and doing some soul-searching."

He opened the metal gate of the tennis court, then followed. They both put their jackets and racket covers at the side, then began a slow and gentle volley. After a few minutes, he asked her if she was ready for a real game and whether or not she would like to serve first. She said he should begin, so he did.

"Love all. Ball one."

ᴗː∾

Sheriff Stone and Deputy Powell left Crested Butte and started toward Gunnison. They talked about the case, the weather, and the upcoming balloon festival. As they approached the Roaring Judy turn-off, they could see that Willis Miller's truck was still parked along the side. There was the chance that he might have remembered something about the previous Friday.

They also wanted to verify what Kate told them about seeing him there. Stone reckoned that if she were telling the truth about one thing, it might follow that she had told the truth about other things. On the other hand, one lie might indicate other lies. In any event, the two men agreed that it would be well worth their time to talk to Miller.

They had no trouble finding Willis Miller. He was in the parking lot loading his fishing tackle and preparing to leave. He seemed very happy to see them and immediately showed them his catch of the day. He offered them each a fish, but they declined politely. Eventually, they got to the point of their stopping by to see him.

"Did you come up with anything else for me?" Stone asked.

"Yes sir, Sheriff. I certainly did. I knew there was something else that I wanted to mention to you, but it plumb slipped my mind that day, then slipped my mind once or twice more whenever I got ready to phone you."

"What is it, Mr. Miller? I'd like to hear it," he encouraged the older man.

"The ladies," he answered directly.

"Ladies?"

"I saw the ladies buzzing around Big Jim that day. He was a mighty lucky man to have such good lookin' ones hangin' all around."

"Do you know them or could you at least describe them?"

"Sure, Sheriff Stone. I didn't know the one, kinda small and pretty. She asked me if I knew where Big Jim might be fishing."

"That would be Kate Mason, huh, Boss?" Powell suggested.

"And the other one?" the Sheriff waited anxiously.

"Why it was Jasper Wilson's wife, Voni. I remember I told you that he was still sitting there in his Blazer when I left, but I was confused. It was her I saw in his old car. My mind plays tricks on me sometimes. He must have left just a minute or two before she got here. One minute he was there; I started packing up my truck, and the next minute she was there."

"Now try and think, was Mrs. Wilson still here when the next lady arrived?" he asked as carefully as he could.

"I do believe she was," he replied thoughtfully.

19

Early Friday evening, the sun was setting beyond the mountains of Red River, New Mexico. Although the summer day would linger, by seven o'clock the square dancers were starting to arrive at the Community Center to participate at the "Southwest square dance capital." Fiddle players could be heard tuning their instruments. Guitarists strummed absently, and there was an audible cymbals crash. Sounds of the preparation could be heard the length of Main Street.

Buck Hayden walked out on the balcony of the two-story motel and leaned against the railing. From that vantage point, he could watch the costumed dancers making their way to the Center. They walked in pairs or in foursomes, always in matching clothes. He was surprised to see how old most of the dancers were. There were as many folks with grey hair as those with brown. A large percentage of the men, he noticed, had no hair at all.

The women were more interesting to look at as far as he was concerned. He suspected that they all had their hair done at the same beauty shop because there was a certain similarity to all of their styles. Their hair was puffed and teased out in a way that reminded him of old-fashioned pictures he had seen of the styles of the 50s and 60s. One lady walked by with her hair piled up so high, he understood what the "beehive" was. He wondered if they were ever able to comb through the stacks.

He did like the way they dressed. Invariably the women's dresses matched their male partner's shirts, and the various designs and colorful combinations made for interesting watching. He particularly liked the red and white checkered dresses that matched the men's red and white shirts; but as he was watching, a foursome in impressive blue and gold outfits strolled passed. Buck noticed that many of the ladies wore their skirts a little too short for the age and the shape of their legs. Some were down right disgusting, he thought.

The petticoats sashayed from to side to side as the ladies walked toward the dance hall. Each step accentuated the swing of the wide hips. He looked on in fascination as well as curiosity. He was certain some of the more elderly women would be referred to as "old dollies" anywhere else. Still he was eagerly looking forward to seeing the dances. There would be standing-room only, he knew, if he did not get a move on and get down there.

⌣∶∾

There was a message on Sheriff Stone's desk when he returned that evening. It was from Charlie at the landfill. It said something to the effect that the Sheriff must be living right, for during the first few minutes that Charlie started looking through the refuse with the metal detector, the .22 had turned up. Charlie was making arrangements for someone in the Crested Butte Marshal's Office to take the weapon to Stone first thing in the morning. Stone looked at the good news, then remembered that it would mean another Saturday at work.

He picked up the telephone thinking that he would call the Wilson house. He'd ask Mrs. Wilson to surrender her handgun, now that an eyewitness had placed her at the crime scene. Then, he remembered Yvonne Wilson's fondness for bingo on Friday night. Without a doubt, she would be at the V.F.W. Hall and not at home, he told himself. He would get the gun from her in the morning, he decided. After all, he had to come into work anyway to await the other delivery.

He wondered if Powell planned to work the weekend also. The young officer was turning into a first-rate detective, he acknowledged. In spite of the difference in their ages, he enjoyed the junior man's company. He liked having another sounding board when he was thinking out loud. Besides, the more he found himself talking to himself, the more he remembered Willis Miller. It would not do for the local citizens to start making comparisons.

Recalling what Miller said about seeing Yvonne Wilson and Kate Mason at the Roaring Judy at the same time, he was perplexed to figure out why Kate had not mentioned seeing the other woman. It would have helped to verify the validity of her statement. He wondered if the fact had merely slipped her mind or if there was another reason she did not want him to know that the Wilson woman was there when she was. Could it be, he asked himself, that Mrs. Wilson had seen the crime?

He closed his eyes very tightly and tried to recall everything that Yvonne Wilson had told him about that Friday. Immediately, he opened his eyes and clenched his teeth hard. He was angry. He distinctly remember that she had told him that she had NOT seen Jim Clancy that day. Now, he was alert. He was well aware that there might be other lies as well. He planned to pull the Wilson file as soon as he returned to the office in the morning. In the meantime, he wanted to get home to his family. He had promised them that they would all go out to dinner after work. By now, he grimaced as he noticed the time, they would be starving.

~:~

It was almost eight o'clock by the time Marva Lee returned from the Safeway supermarket. She enjoyed doing her shopping after work on Fridays. That left her free to pursue her other pastimes and do housework and gardening on the weekends. Working a full-time job was finally starting to become a strain on her physically. She knew that most of her teacher friends and other chums had long since retired. She considered also that the upkeep of the large house might be becoming too much of a chore for her, yet she could not see herself moving anywhere else. She owned too much furniture to consider moving to the senior center or even to a townhouse. There was no way in the world that she would part with the furniture she had spent a lifetime collecting.

She was just taking in the first bag of groceries when she noticed the familiar newspaper bundle on her step. Willis Miller had been there and had left her a beautiful trout. She sighed as she picked up the gift and placed it in the kitchen sink. She hoped that it would keep one more day because she had already eaten before going to the store. If he would ever tell her in advance that he was bringing something over, she knew she would appreciate knowing.

After all the years that she had known Willis, however, she knew that he would probably never change, not one iota. His constant babbling to his departed friends was enough to drive any sane person to distraction, but she noted, when he shup up, he could be an interesting fellow. It was just a shame that his memory was so defective. She wondered how many times in the past she had called him to come over and do some work, and he had forgotten to come, leaving her waiting for him. She wished she had a nickel for every time.

She finished putting away the groceries and took a can of Coke Classic out of the refrigerator. She poured herself a Coke and thought about Willis Miller again. She wondered if he would be at the bingo game with half of the other folks in town. As she pictured the game in her mind, Marva Lee was reminded of Yvonne Wilson.

⋌⋅⋋

For the first time in a long time, Yvonne Wilson did not want to go to bingo. She was depressed. She believed that she needed a change of scenery. Maybe, she considered, she could talk Jasper into a little trip to Lake Tahoe. Recalling her current gambling debts, she decided that it would be easier to talk him into that New England tour he was always talking about. She guessed that she wouldn't mind a nice, long trip back East, away from the nosey Sheriff Stone.

That guy had some nerve, Voni admitted to herself. He had done everything but come right out and ask her if she were sleeping with Clancy, and that information certainly was not any of his business. Also, she wondered how long it would be before the Mason woman told him that she had seen Voni at the Roaring Judy. Then, Stone would know for certain that she had lied to him. She definitely needed to get out of town and soon.

Yvonne knew what she needed was cash. Her checking account was almost flat, but somewhere in Jasper's chest of drawers, he kept a savings account pass book. If she could send him out of the house for a short while, Voni knew that it would not take her long to locate it. Fixing her hair and applying more makeup, she sauntered downstairs to talk to her husband.

As usual, Jasper was at the kitchen table looking over blueprints and maps of the Kebler Pass Project. He did not even look up from his work as she came in the room, so she pouted before she spoke.

"Jasper, Honey. You know I am just craving some good ice cream. 'Member that mocha fudge you bought last week that was so good? You want a dish?" she asked sweetly knowing full well that there was no ice cream in the house.

"Sure, Darlin', if you're having some," he answered as he looked up from his work.

"Just be a minute, Sugar," she cooed, removing two bowls from the cabinet and put out two spoons beside them. Then she went to the freezer and made a big show of looking for the missing ice cream.

"Now, don't that beat all! I could have sworn there was some ice cream left," she lied. "Gotta be here somewhere," she expressed her unhappiness and false confusion.

"Want me to take a look?" the man offered.

"No. No sense in doing that. It's just not my night. First this blasted headache kept me from bingo, and now I had my mouth all set for that mocha fudge. Maybe I'll just go on back to bed and lie down some more." she complained.

"I can run out and get the ice cream if you want," Jasper offered.

"No. Thank you, Darlin', it would be such a bother for you to go to the store. I just couldn't ask...well, truth is I really do want...no, I couldn't possibly ask you to get it," the woman whimpered as she spoke.

"That's OK. I really don't mind. Quik-Shop should still be open. I'll be right back," he confirmed as he got up from the table and put on his jacket.

"Maybe you ought to take another one of those aspirin while I'm out," he suggested kindly.

Yvonne smiled at the man and nodded slowly as she watched him go out of the door to the garage. The minute he pulled out of the driveway, like lightning, she dashed back up the stairs to look for the bank book!

For several minutes, she felt through the man's personal clothing. She was about to give up when her hand touched something in the drawer behind the man's sweaters. She pulled the box out of the drawer, but she did not need to open it to know what it was. It was the box that held her .22. She wondered how Jasper had managed to get it and move it to his things without her knowledge. She remembered very well that she had last had that gun in her purse, just in case...

110

The loud music vibrated the crowded Community Center in Red River. The monotone sing-song voice of the square dance caller commanded the dancers around the floor:

"Left hand lady with the left hand round, all join circle and go to town. Gents to the center and take a bow; ya got there quick, but you don't know how. Swing that corner lady round, she's the prettiest gal you've ever found. Now, take your partner a-la-main left and promenade!"

Buck Hayden watched the whirling twirling colors of the many dance costumes. It was like a living kaleidoscope on the floor. He was impressed by the coordination of the various routines and with the precision of the dancers. They danced as though they had done the routine one hundred times before. Then, he laughed to himself as he said under his breath, "Judging from some of their ages, they probably have done it 100 times."

Looking around to see if anyone else had heard his remark, he was relieved to see that no one else was paying any attention to him. All eyes were on the spry folks on the dance floor.

The place was warming up as the people packed inside to get a better view. He was starting to feel a little closed-in and crowded. Maybe, he told himself, it would be a good time to take a stroll up the street and cool off. He decided he could walk up the street to the Black Mountain Playhouse and play some of the video games in the arcade. He loved that place. He could also see if there were any roller skaters and grab a snack as well. He was not interested in their indoor miniature golf.

He had not walked vary far from the Center when he was stopped by an officer from the New Mexico State Highway Patrol.

⌇⁚⁓

Sheriff Stone was awakened from a deep sleep by his dispatcher. The report was confirmed, and the dispatcher knew that the Sheriff would want the information immediately: Buck Hayden had been arrested in Red River, New Mexico, and the Bronco had been recovered. Hayden would be returned to Gunnison County on Monday.

Stone fell back on his pillow and smiled into the darkness.

20

Sheriff Stone arrived at his office at eight o'clock Saturday morning. Deputy Powell was already there and had a pot of coffee ready. The dispatcher had also let Powell know about Hayden's capture, so he had been as eager as his boss to get to work on the Clancy case. The lawmen went over the details of the report that had been transmitted to their headquarters.

It seemed that the motel manager had been suspicious of Buck and had asked the local law enforcement office to find out if there was anything on the man or the Bronco. It had not taken the locals long to find out that the vehicle was on the APB issued from Colorado. The State Highway Patrol was given the task of staking out the man's room and watching for his return. Soon, they saw a man matching the motel manager's description.

The arrest had been an easy one. The man offered no resistance. He was armed with a small knife that he carried in his boot, but there was no trouble. The New Mexico authorities were notifying the Chavez family that their truck had been safely recovered. Buck Hayden would be returned to Gunnison County for questioning.

That was all good news for Stone and Powell. Finally, they would get some answers about what happened between Clancy and Hayden that day. The disgruntled employee had obviously burglarized the Clancy cabin, but neither of the lawmen believed that there was evidence to suggest that Hayden shot the man. Buck Hayden certainly had a motive, but the officers did not see that there was any connection to the murder weapon or to the crime scene, unless he wore a size ten Roper. They knew they would have more answers on Monday.

As the men went over the facts in the case, they checked the time. Stone wanted to telephone the Wilsons as soon as it was nine. After awhile, Stone made the call.

"Good morning, Mr. Wilson. This is Sheriff Stone. Sorry to disturb you so early," he apologized.

"No problem, Sheriff, I'm an early riser. What can I do for you?" Jasper Wilson asked.

"I find that your wife owns a .22 handgun. It's registered in her name. I would like to have a look at that gun today, and I was wondering if you would mind dropping it by my office?"

"Well, I don't know, Sheriff. My wife is still asleep..."

"I can get a search warrant and come over there if need be," Stone told him with only the slightest edge of a threat in his tone.

"No, sir, that won't be necessary," Wilson answered quickly.

"Could I expect you here within an hour, shall we say?" the Sheriff inquired.

"Yes, sir. If there are complications, I'll call you."

"I appreciate that, Mr. Wilson," the officer replied as he hung up the phone.

Sheriff Stone sat quietly just looking at the timeline on his desk in front of him. He looked at Powell and scowled the scowl that Tim Powell had learned meant that the senior man was mentally computing some special aspect of the investigation. He waited for the older man to speak first when he saw that look.

After what must have been five or ten minutes, Stone looked up at Powell and scowled again. Powell wished that there was a mirror in the room so that he could show the Sheriff how he looked when he made that face. Then, after he thought about it, he was glad there was not a mirror to tempt him into doing something that probably would cost him his job. He liked his job.

Finally Stone spoke, "Wilson hinted that there might be complications of some sort about bringing in the gun. You don't suppose he thinks his wife has pitched that one too?"

"No way, sir," Powell reassured him. "He probably just meant that his wife might have put it away somewhere and forgotten where. Something simple like that."

"I certainly hope you are right. There are dozens of places around here to ditch a pistol so that it would never be found," Stone reminded him.

"If it's not the murder weapon, they have nothing to fear. No reason at all why they shouldn't cooperate."

"That's right, Powell. Of course, they might not know just how accurate Ballistics can be. They could be willing to take a chance. We know for a fact that one person in the family is a compulsive gambler."

"Boss, even if the gun has been thoroughly cleaned, the markings on the slug and from the barrel are going to tell the story. Surely they've seen enough crime shows to know that."

"I don't know, Powell. We'll have to wait and see."

⌣∶∾

Jasper Wilson did not want to wait around the house. He needed to get to the Kebler Pass Project. This would be one time that Yvonne would have to handle matters on her own. He no longer had the time if he were going to try and save his business. He woke her up before he left, but she was so groggy that she did not seem to hear or understand a word he said. He kissed the top of her head and left.

Wilson was half way to Crested Butte when he remembered about Sheriff Stone. He stopped at Three Rivers Outfitters and used their phone to let Stone know that he could not find the pistol.

⌣∶∾

"Does that beat all or what?" Stone practically yelled at the younger officer. The scowl was back. "We're gonna get that warrant and toss the place upside down. We'll get the Ropers too if they're still around," he was determined.

"Easy, Boss. Maybe Mrs. Wilson can come up with it. Why don't we just go on over there?"

"No, Powell. We're going with a warrant as soon as we can get it. We're not going to be caught short on this one. People can't just be misplacing weapons! Not in my county!"

Stone was as animated as the Deputy had ever seen him. He knew the long hours that the Sheriff was putting in on the case. He just wished that there would be a major break instead of so many convoluted trails. He was just about to go back to his own office when a courier arrived from Crested Butte. The Sheriff opened the package; it was Kate Mason's gun, ready to go to Ballistics.

Dr. Kellog finished examining Judge Winfield, then waited for the obese man to get dressed. While he waited for Winfield, he looked over the results of the tests he had run on the large man. The weight was unbelievable, and he could only guess at the man's stamina. Yet, as he looked at the numbers, he could see that the attorney was in no danger of any immediate health problem other than a bothersome case of gastroenteritis. His cholesterol was within normal limits, though how, the physician had no idea.

On paper, except for the obvious weight problem, Grant Winfield was as strong as an ox. The liver, kidneys, all the urine and blood work appeared to be normal. One just could never tell, the doctor reminded himself.

For a few moments his mind flashed to another of his patients, Kate Mason. She appeared to be so healthy and had good coloring and vitality, but she was a walking timebomb. Her most recent blood count worried him. There was not a doubt in his mind that her time was extremely limited. He hinted that fact to her at each visit, but he could never come right out and tell her she might have only weeks or months to live. He suspected that she knew that fact, though, as the doctor she was seeing in Denver was one of the best.

All he could do for the woman was to increase her medication dosage and try to talk her into a complete transfusion, which so far she had been unwilling to do. As long as the weather stayed nice, and she got plenty of fresh air and exercise, her time would be extended. He knew from experience, however, the colder winter flu season would be devastating. She simply would no longer have the resistance to ward off germs. She would be as helpless as someone standing in front of a locomotive trying to stop the train with a toothpick.

It really did not seem fair. She was a lovely and charming woman who had obviously taken care of herself throughout her life. She was well-educated and becoming a respected member of the community. Dr. Kellog saw very little hope for her, short of a miracle.

Grant Winfield tapped on the inner office door, then he went in to review his case with the doctor. He could instantly see that the M.D. had a look of gloom and doom on his face. He assumed that he must have failed an important test.

"It's OK, Doc. You can tell me. How long have I got?" He asked somberly.

"Ah, Winfield. How long indeed?" he replied cheerfully. "I would say another twenty years if you behave and always cross the street at the crosswalk!"

"I don't understand," the big man spoke. "You looked so serious when I walked in. I thought I must need a bypass or something."

"Nope. You're in great shape under that mountain of unnecessary weight you're toting around. It's not good for you at all," the doctor scolded.

"The pain I was having?"

"Heartburn. Too many tacos, too many hot dogs, etc. I am going to have my dietician set up an appointment with you for the first part of next week. We're going to put you on a diet. Believe me, you'll feel a lot better."

"I don't know, Doc," the man sounded hesitant.

"Ah, come on. You'll love it. It's going to take some willpower, and effort over time, but hopefully you will be able to lose 100 or 150 pounds before we have to get serious."

"Well, if it will help make this pain go away, I guess I'm ready to give it a try. At least it will get Marva Lee to quit nagging me!"

⌣:∾

Miss Marva Lee Linden was already at work in her garden. There seemed to be no end to the damage she kept finding. The storm had taken more of a toll on her plants than she had first thought. Many little stems were snapped in such a way that the plants were dying. She was very disappointed as she trimmed and carried the clippings and debris to her large trash barrel.

Some of the plants in her garden were doing exceptionally well, though, she noted. All of the shrubs along her east wall were lush and green, the best they had ever been. She knew the reason why, but she had not told anyone her secret for successful gardening. She especially did not want Willis Miller to know as he might be offended knowing how he was always chattering about burials and digging graves and such.

The fact was that she buried all of the fish heads and extra fish Willis gave her. She put the scraps right into the ground. She sometimes ate the fish because all the magazines said that fish was supposed to be good for a person, but mostly, she planted them. Her shrubs obviously enjoyed the treat. She appreciated the free source of fertilizer.

She wondered how Judge Winfield was doing at his appointment with Dr. Kellog. She hoped that Kellog would put a real scare into the fat man for his own good. As often as she had been angered and disgusted with the man, she still felt a great deal of kindredness for him. He had provided her with a very good job over the years. She, in turn, had been as efficient as humanly possible. They had worked well together for a long time.

She continued cleaning up her garden. Her petunias needed insecticide. The geraniums that were still standing after the storm looked as if the previous night had been much too cold for them; they would have to be repotted and taken inside. That meant rounding up the pots from the workshed and scrubbing them out before the move was made. The grapevines needed to be retied again. The garden was a never ending amount of chores, but she loved it.

Lawn mowing she could do without and did. The small patch of grass in front of her house was mowed by a neighbor boy for a few dollars a week. He also took care of the little well-house. A wellhouse the size of a doghouse could be found in front of almost every home in that part of Gunnison. By using the pump from the runoff water in the narrow ditch, the citizens could have free water for their yards. The idea was good, but the hoses and pipes and well houses were a constant untidy mess from one house to the next. No one in the city had come up with an acceptable alternative. Several home owners were creative and made little water wheels and other decorative items along the tiny stream.

Marva Lee confined her creativity to her small garden plots. She was very proud of the mixture of flowers and vegetables she grew every year. She loved her flowers, but the practical side of her nature insisted that she also grow tomatoes and cucumbers. She had a row of leaf lettuce and two short rows of radishes and onions as well. As long as the weather held, Marva Lee expected to keep harvesting a good crop. She wondered if the Judge just might enjoy some fresh salad items. She would take some in to him on Monday morning.

117

Sheriff Stone and Deputy Powell stood outside the Wilson house knocking on the door. After several minutes, a very sleepy-looking Yvonne Wilson answered the door and let them in. At first, she acted very embarrassed to be seen without her makeup on and her hair uncombed. She held her fluffy robe around her as though she could try and hide within it.

Powell listened to the woman as she told them to come in and watched them as they took out their search warrant. He thought she looked 100 percent better without all of the makeup on her face. She was actually quite pretty. Her hair was another story. He was shocked at the way her hair stood out. It reminded him of a cartoon he saw as a child, the one in which a cat somehow gets hold of a live electric wire.

Yvonne Wilson listened while the Sheriff explained that he really needed to see the gun and any pair of Roper boots that her husband might have.

21

Yvonne Wilson asked the lawmen to sit down for a minute while she went upstairs to put on some clothes. They assured her that they did not mind waiting a few minutes, but urged her to hurry. After the woman left the room, the officers talked.

"How long do you think she'll take, Sheriff?" Powell asked.

"Your guess is as good as mine. This isn't some big city like L.A. The lady is a local citizen; we all know each other. Doesn't seem right nor decent not to let her go put on something more suitable. I just hope she doesn't take all day," Stone spoke wishfully.

"This could take some time," Powell agreed remembering the wildness of her hair.

Yvonne Wilson went in her bedroom and shut the door. She felt the panic of fear in the pit of her stomach as she tried to recall something Jasper had told her before he left for work that morning. She had been too sleepy to understand what he was saying at the time, but it had been something about Stone. She wondered if she should call her husband at work.

She looked at her watch and realized that the officers, as gentlemanly as they were, would not be willing to wait long, so she quickly pulled on a pair of velour jogging pants and matching top. The soft material felt good as she hurried to the sink to wash her face. She brushed her teeth and combed her hair straight back and tied it with a ribbon. She only had time to add some lipstick before rushing to look for the gun.

Yvonne pulled open the same drawer of Jasper's cabinet that she had opened the night before. Reaching far to the back of the drawer, she could feel the edge of the box. She pulled the small box out and knew right away that the gun was not inside. It should have been much heavier. Putting the box on the bed, she slapped her cheeks slightly to bring their color, then went back downstairs to join the men.

Both Stone and Powell were pleased to see Mrs. Wilson return so promptly. They had anticipated that she would need at least half an hour to be presentable, so they appreciated her haste. They both also noticed that she really was a very attractive woman.

She smiled at them as she came back into the room. Coffee was offered, but the officers declined. They needed to get back to work, they insisted, as they reminded her that they were just there to pick up the gun and a pair of Ropers if Wilson owned any.

"Oh, Sheriff Stone. I am more than sorry about all of this. I usually keep that gun in its box in my night stand. I get nervous when Jasper works late," she explained.

"That's fine, ma'am. It's legally registered," Stone assured her.

"No. There's a problem. The gun is not in the box. I think it's in the Blazer. I used to drive that truck the most, and I sometimes got scared if I was out on the road by myself. You know how far it is between houses on some stretches of road."

Stone agreed with the sparse population but failed to see what that had to do with the matter at hand.

"Jasper took the Blazer up to Kebler Pass this morning. See?" She looked at them helplessly. "I'm stuck here all day with the old car since he needs 4-wheel drive up there," she whined.

Stone turned to Powell and watched the younger man roll his eyes in consternation. The Sheriff did not say anything for a moment.

"Ma'am, we would still like to look at your husband's boots if there are any here," Stone sounded almost sarcastic.

"Why certainly," she answered brightly. "I know there's a pair in the closet by the back door. Let me get them for you. You'll want a bag to take them in," she added.

Powell spoke for the Sheriff, "We'll just take a look at them first, ma'am, if you don't mind." He wanted to see if they were a size 10 before he bothered to have them tested.

"Here they are, brand new!" she announced proudly as she handed the well-shined boots to the junior officer.

Powell looked them over and was pleased to see that the size showed clearly. They were a size 10.

"Ma'am, we'll be writing you a receipt for these. We need to take them into the lab."

"Now, Mrs. Wilson, about the gun," Sheriff Stone spoke sternly. "You can see that I have a warrant to search this place from top to bottom. It won't be a pretty sight having us dig through everything you own," he hesitated as he heard her gasp.

"We must have that gun to make a comparison test, and now you tell us the gun is not here. Can you get ahold of your husband and have him return and bring in the gun?"

"Yes, Sheriff. I can phone up there, but he may be already at the construction site. He has a radio, but with all the earth moving equipment and such making noise, he doesn't always hear the pager right away."

"I am going to give you exactly one hour to contact him. If he has not called me or returned to my office in person, I am going to send an entire unit over here to search the premises. We'll go over this place with a fine-toothed comb. I guarantee, you will not like it," he paused and let the warning sink in.

"Furthermore, I will contact the Marshal up there to arrest your husband and hold him for interfering with police business. I spoke to Mr. Wilson earlier and told him at that time how much we needed his cooperation. No more excuses!"

The woman stared at him as though she were seeing him for the first time. His badge looked bigger than she remembered. The County Sheriff was a force to be reckoned with.

"One hour?" she asked.

"One hour," Stone repeated.

Sheriff Stone and Deputy Powell left the house and returned to the Sheriff's Office. Stone told his deputy to notify a unit team to prepare to execute a search warrant. He wanted plenty of men so that the job would go as quickly as possible. He also telephoned the lab and told them he would be bringing a pair of Ropers in to compare for the Clancy case. They told him to Bring them in straight away as they had some free time and could examine them immediately.

"Willis Miller has already told us that he saw Jasper Wilson having an argument with Clancy. Don't you believe him, Boss?" the younger man questioned.

"Of course I do, Powell, but would a jury? The boot size gives us just that much more. The actual boot would be even better."

Why don't we just arrest him and bring him in? Let's ask him

121

straight out."

"Powell, I want to be holding as many aces as possible when we do make the arrest. I don't want any foul-ups or slip-throughs. We've worked too hard on this case."

"You're right, Boss. Mrs. Wilson isn't exactly lily-white either. Miller says she was there, but there are not footprints that even come close to implicating her and no known motive. She just happens to own a .22 which may have or may not have been at Jasper's disposal," the young man summarized.

"We still have to consider Kate Mason and Buck Hayden as well," Stone reminded Powell. "Mason was there; she has the right type of gun—which she tried to dispose of after the murder. So far, we just have not found the motive, but I can feel in my bones that it is a-comin'." The Sheriff sounded more cheerful than he had in some time.

"We'll have Buck here Monday," Powell added.

"That's right. Peek is coming back in about then too. We can reunite those former roommates right here in a cell."

They spoke for a few more minutes then turned their attention to other police matters while they waited for the deadline they had given the Wilsons.

⌐∴∾

Yvonne Wilson dialed the Kebler Pass Project. Her hands were shaking as she held the telephone and waited for Jasper to come on line. She chewed her lower lip scrapping the vivid polish away and onto her teeth. She needed to know where the pistol was. While she waited, she wished that the night before she had thought to look inside the box. She had been so intent on finding the bank book, that the money was the only thing on her mind.

She did find the book. It was not hidden at all; it was on the desk in plain sight in Jasper's small study. She took the book, though, and put it under a kleenex box on her night stand. It was not until later, when she was eating ice cream with her husband that she remembered that the bank would not be open until Monday. There was no way Yvonne Wilson would leave town without money.

While she continued to wait on the phone, she thought about the gun. Mentally, she scolded herself for having been so careless with the weapon. She should have kept the gun in her purse or in

122

its box. Probably, she surmised, she should have gotten rid of it. It was dangerous.

Finally, her husband answered. She explained the situation to him and told him how angry Sheriff Stone had sounded. He seemed to understand the urgency of the situation and assured her that he would soon be in touch with Stone. In the meantime, he informed her, he would go back out to the Blazer and see if the gun was there.

~:~

While Sheriff Stone and Deputy Powell waited in the police headquarters, a steady stream of traffic began to pass by their building on Highway 50. Motorists were coming into town by the hundreds, as they made their way to the opening of the Second Annual Balloon Festival in Crested Butte. Gunnison would be just a stopover for the many people on their way to see the highly publicized event. As the lawmen watched the crowds pouring into town, they were just as glad that they were not hosting the activity. It would mean a lot of overtime.

~:~

Jeff Harper was looking forward to the Balloon Festival as he waited for Kate at her apartment. He had read that the festival would be the largest of its kind in Colorado, and he was excited about it. The idea of hot air ballooning was a favorite of his ever since he attended a larger such event in Albuquerque, New Mexico when he was younger.

He wanted to show Kate around the field of balloons so that she would appreciate their simplicity and beauty even before the scheduled mass ascension on Sunday morning. He knew that sight would be impressive, but he wanted to teach her more about the colorful giants.

For some reason he could not understand completely, he loved talking to Kate. She was such a good listener and eager to learn new things, he guessed that was what drew him to her. Her zest for life inspired him to try harder in his own work. Her always pleasant manner was comforting. At least it had been, he realized, until she had started talking about the will and dying. He did not want that

123

subject to come up again. He felt particularly uncomfortable knowing that he was her beneficiary for he did not want her to think that he was spending time with her because of that.

Soon, he knew, he would have to tell her his big news. He was not certain what she would think about his plans, so he wanted to wait a few days before telling her the details of his phone call from Washington. He had hinted to her before that there might be hope of a promotion, but he had not explained the impact that might have on their relationship. He had so many things he wanted to say to her.

After a few minutes, Kate was ready, and they left her small apartment for the International Balloon Field south of the village. There were plenty of parking attendants on duty to assist with the traffic. Everything seemed to be very well-organized to meet the needs of the enormous crowd. The cars were directed into the rows along the southern end of the field; and within a few minutes, Kate and Harper were walking through the admissions gate and into the area proper.

There was every kind of food booth set up along the main entrance gate. Some vendors sold doughnuts and coffee; others offered more exotic fare such as breakfast burritos, and teriyaki-on-a-stick. There was something for everyone. Hot chocolate and hot apple cider booths seemed to have the longest lines in front of their stands. As the day warmed up, the cold drink vendors would increase their business.

Jeff Harper asked his companion, "Would you like something? We could get it since we're right here."

"It's up to you. I'm OK, really. Maybe something later?" she answered sweetly.

"All right," the young man agreed. "Let's go on out and have a closer look at those floaters!"

22

The giant balloons were in various stages of inflation as Kate and Harper entered the expansive International Balloon Park. The occasional roar of the multiple burners was an awesome sound in the otherwise still morning as the thin cool air of the high altitude seemed to magnify the raspy sound. The large crowd of sightseers moved in among the many balloons in quiet awe.

"Jeff, this is incredible! I had no idea that the balloons were so large. Whenever I've seen one in the air, I guess I was fooled by the perspective." She looked as happy as a little child at a carnival.

"They're great, aren't they?" he acknowledged. "I've only been up in one, but it was a great feeling. You can't believe how light you feel up there."

"Oh, I believe you. That's probably why they are called 'lighter than air,'" she teased him.

They walked further into the throng of onlookers toward the center of the field. She asked him whether or not the balloons would be launching, but he told her they would not. This morning, he explained, would just be a series of tethered inflations and checking of equipment. Very early the next morning, he commented, when the air was extremely cool just after dawn, the balloons would be launched in an orderly mass ascension.

While they stood watching the balloonists, pilots, and chase crews practice, Harper described some of the balloon features and facts to her:

"The hot air balloons have three major components: the basket, the burner, and the envelope, the name for the air bag itself. The envelope is a tough, highly durable nylon fabric which is coated with polyurethane to make it airtight. The coating also helps protect the material from the harmful rays of the sun. The frame itself is basically a nylon webbing."

Kate asked questions about the size of the balloon, and Harper explained, "Most of these balloons are Class 6 or Class 7. That's pretty standard. A 6 can carry two people in the basket, but a 7 can take three. A Class 7 is about 55 feet in diameter and has a volume of around 77,500 cubic feet."

She was very impressed with his scientific interest in the sport as he continued telling her about the principles involved in the flight. He told how the envelopes were laid out on the ground first and pointed one out to her on the field. Then he took her to where a team was beginning to fill their craft.

They stood and watched the busy team work on filling the envelope. Cold air was pumped into the big nylon structure by means of a large gasoline engine-powered fan at the bottom of the balloon. The air was heated with a propane gas burner, the same burners that they heard when they first arrived at the field. Harper reminded her that hot air rises only if there is a significant difference between the temperature inside the balloon and the cold air on the outside. That was one reason, he noted, that pilots liked the early morning hours the best.

As the air inside the inflated structure began to heat up, Harper and Kate could see that the ground crew was struggling to keep the monstrous structure tethered. The crew strained to hold the hot air balloon in check.

"How on earth do they steer these things once they get them up there? There doesn't seem to be much in the way of control." She hoped Harper knew the answer.

"You are absolutely right. There aren't many steering options. The pilot has to know the wind currents and adjust his altitude constantly to catch the desired prevailing direction. Of course, they don't go up at all if the wind is too strong."

"Like what Jeff?" Kate was curious.

"I've heard some pilots say that about 4 to 6 mph is perfect. I think that they also launch if it's up to 8 mph, doubtful they would try it in 10 or 12. They need plenty of visibility too."

"How do they know how high they are?"

Harper led her closer to one of the wicker baskets and asked the man attending to the basket if he would mind letting them look at the instrument panel. With the congenial man's permission, the young scientist pointed out the altimeter to her. He also showed her the gauge that would indicate the rate of climb. Then, he indicated where the fuel tank was and explained that the balloon's length of flight often depended on just how much fuel it could carry.

"I can't wait to see them all flying," she spoke enthusiastically. "They're so beautiful! I just love all of the colors."

"You think these are nice, let me take you to the other side of the field where they are preparing the ones that are going to take part in a 'shapes rodeo.'"

"Shapes rodeo? I can't imagine..." she started to say, but stopped as he took her by the hand and began to lead her quickly across the field.

"There!" he announced. "The shapes!"

In front of them was a wide variety of hot air balloons that looked like anything except balloons. They were true creations of fantasy and humor. There was an enormous cow, an airplane, a large clown, and a soft drink can. There were so many whimsical shapes that Kate clapped her hands and jumped up a bit in delight. She couldn't ever remember seeing anything like it.

"It's wonderful! Just wonderful," she exclaimed as she turned and gave him a hearty hug. "Thank you so much for bringing me."

"I knew you would like it," he replied. "Tomorrow morning is going to be even better. Besides all of the balloons, there will be skydivers and parachutists. All kinds of stunt flyers are in town for the two weeks of festivities."

"It's marvelous." She continued to be awed by the sheer numbers gathered on the field.

"Well, how about it? Will you join me for the 'Dawn Patrol' tomorrow?" he inquired.

"I would love to, I really would," she answered and smiled into his happy face.

⌒∴∾

Jasper Wilson walked back out to his Blazer. He opened the glove compartment and took out the gun. It looked so small in his large hand that he had to remind himself how deadly a pistol can be. He did not know if it were loaded or not, but he did not want to take any chances. As he looked at the weapon, he knew that the

127

Sheriff must have reason to think that the gun was the one that killed Clancy.

Wilson told himself that if Stone wanted to see their gun, it could only mean that he suspected that one of them had murdered Big Jim. He knew that Ballistics would be able to determine whether or not the gun had fired the fatal shot. What would happen then, he could only guess.

He went back into the little trailer house that served as their office at the site. He stood looking out on the great Kebler Pass and envisioned once again the projected amusement park he and Big Jim had planned there so many months ago. He watched the giant earth movers and bulldozers clearing the land, stripping away acre after acre of beautiful forest, and he was momentarily sickened.

He knew it had been greed and pure greed only that had led him into his business deal with Clancy. He had not cared what happened to the land nor the environment when they began. He had merely been looking for additional riches to keep his wife satisfied. It had seemed impossible though. The more he gave her, the more she wanted. It wasn't that she was nasty about it or anything, it was as though her needs were like a large paper bag with no bottom in it. Whatever he gave her simply fell on through the opening. Nothing remained, just a great emptiness.

He had provided for her the best way he knew how through all of their married years. He really did not know what he should have done differently. There was just some great hunger in the woman that nothing seemed to help. Maybe she needed to see a professional, he considered.

Even in death, Jim Clancy was still causing trouble for those who knew him. To Jasper Wilson it just did not seem right. There had to be an end to it sometime.

He picked up the telephone and called Sheriff Stone in Gunnison. He told the officer that he had the gun with him, and that he would return to the city with it as soon as possible. He said he would leave immediately and should be at Stone's office within forty minutes or so. As he hung up after talking to the lawman, he made another major decision; all work on the Kebler Pass Project would cease.

Jasper Wilson vowed to reforest the land if it took every cent he had.

Sheriff Stone breathed a sigh of relief. He notified the search unit to stand down. There would be no need to go to the Wilson house after all. Everyone was happy with the news.

Powell knocked on the Sheriff's door and joined him.

"Boss, I understand Wilson is on the way in," the younger man suggested.

"Glad you got the word. I was just going to buzz you. At least that's one little job we won't have to do today. We might get a real day of rest tomorrow after all," he spoke happily.

"I heard the news when I was called downstairs to the lab boys. They had the report on the Roper and wanted me to break the news to you," he waited for the Sheriff's full attention.

"Wilson's boot?"

"His boot, but no match on that pair. Lab says the boot at the scene was not that new. The way the heel print was, they think it had to be from a very old pair," he told his superior.

"Well, it's a setback, but we won't give up. I'm hanging onto this warrant. Wilson may have an old pair we don't know about. Anyway, the gun is far more important right now. With any luck, we'll have something on both guns sometime Monday."

"Yes, sir. One of those guns is going to tell the story," the younger man affirmed. "Right now, I wish it didn't have to be either of those women."

"It doesn't, Powell. It doesn't have to be either one of those ladies. Jasper Wilson could have done it if the gun was in the vehicle with him that day. Remember, Willis Miller told us how upset Wilson was when he saw him," Stone pointed out the fact.

"Boss, do you think that either of the Wilsons would cover for the other in a case like this? Like the Rawlins kid tried to do for her brother?" he asked.

"That remains to be seen, doesn't it? Personally, I can't see Mrs. Wilson taking the heat for anybody. Jasper Wilson's another story. He seems to be a decent sort. Might consider taking the rap for his wife," the Sheriff speculated.

The officers sat and talked and waited for Wilson to arrive with the weapon. They discussed the plans that they had made for Sunday. Stone said he planned to take his family to the Balloon Festival in the early morning. Powell, on the other hand, said that he wanted to just sleep in for once. He thought he might call Linda Lou after lunch and take in a movie that evening.

Finally, almost exactly to the minute as he had promised, Jasper Wilson walked into the Sheriff's Office and handed over the gun.

23

Monday morning was hectic in Sheriff Stone's office. The large crowds in the county over the weekend had resulted in increased traffic and parking citations. Even though the tourists had been well-behaved in general, there was still a mountain of annoying incidents that had to be taken care of. Parking on lawns and blocking driveways around the route to Crested Butte headed the list. There was also a wave of petty shoplifting complaints filed by the local merchants. One or two drunk and disorderlies had spent time in the jail during the night, but all in all, nothing serious had taken place.

Sheriff Stone was pleased that his citizens were not included in the law breaking. He particularly hated to arrest people he knew personally. Besides being downright embarrassing, it was annoying. He thought that they should know better than to create extra work for him.

Deputy Powell came to Stone's office with news.

"Morning, Boss. Just had an interesting conversation with a lady from over at the Clancy business office."

"Oh, yeah?" Stone was curious.

"She just called to let us know that in her Saturday pouch of invoices and checks, there was a cashed payroll check belonging to Buck Hayden. It was cashed in Red River last week."

"Well, I guess we were destined to catch that boy one way or another. The New Mexico troopers just worked a little faster. Lucky for us he hadn't moved on."

"Yes, sir. Dispatcher told me a few minutes ago that we could expect Hayden and escorts to arrive any time," he spoke cheerfully.

"Powell, why don't we go on down to the lab and see what

they have got for us. Might be something?" he added hopefully.

The lawmen entered the small lab and waited for the man in charge. When the technician finished what he was doing, he went to his files and brought out a report that had been completed only a few minutes before. He shared the results with the men.

"Here you are, Sheriff. This summary is being typed right now to be sent up to you, but I can tell you in a nutshell what it says," he offered.

"I'd appreciate that. My desk is piled high with paperwork right now as it is," Stone told him.

"OK. You can see the bottom of this paragraph," he showed the two officers. "We have a perfect match on the shoe at the crime scene and a shoe brought in belonging to Kate Mason. It had microscopic traces of soil from the area as well."

"Those shoes looked perfectly clean to me," Powell interjected.

"Yes, deputy, they were clean, but we inserted a thin probe between the sole and the leather and took the sample."

"Boss, the Mason lady told us she was there," Powell refreshed his memory.

The lab specialist commented, "Kate Mason was definitely at the scene. The hair sample was a perfect match. In fact, she was there at almost the exact time of death. Not only that, but the hair found on the victim had blood on it in such a way that it had to have gotten there as the man was actually still bleeding."

"That's not good," Stone remarked gloomily. "She told us Clancy had no pulse when she touched him."

"No, I would say that the man might well have been alive judging by the blood coating on the strand. If the bleeding could have been stopped, he still would not have had a chance. There was too much damage to the heart according to the medical examiner. That little bullet careened around in there something fierce! Like a pinball!"

"So you are saying that Mason was wrong?" the Sheriff questioned.

"Sheriff Stone, it is very easy for non-medical personnel to panic in such a situation and assume that the victim is already dead. That's not uncommon at all. Been plenty of cases where a person who was merely unconscious or stunned has been buried alive by his attacker. Thinking that the victim is dead, the perpetrator panics. In his haste to get rid of the body as evidence, he buries the poor bloke alive. Happens more than I care to think about," the technician assured them.

"Thanks for your help. Appreciate your working on this, but call me the minute the report is in from Ballistics on the handguns. I need to know right away whether it is Mason's or Wilson's," he reminded the man.

"Yes, sir, Sheriff Stone. You'll know the minute I find out," he assured the officer.

The two lawmen were returning to Stone's office when they heard a commotion in the hallway.

A policeman hurrying up the corridor stopped to tell them, "It's nothing, sir. A little scuffle broke out when the prisoners were being booked."

"Prisoners?"

"Yes, sir. Buck Hayden threw a punch at Ben Peek the moment he came through the door and laid eyes on him! They're still trading insults."

"Hayden wasn't cuffed when he came in?" Stone growled.

"Oh, yes, sir. He was. He just lunged at the guy with his whole body ."

"I see. Tell the Duty Sergeant. I'll be over there to talk to Hayden as soon as they have him tucked in. Make certain that none of his rights get violated. He is a slippery one," Stone warned.

⌣⁖∼

Sunday had been a wonderful day in Crested Butte as far as Kate Mason was concerned. She and Jeff Harper enjoyed themselves all day, from the early morning festivities at the mass ascension balloon launch after dawn to a late afternoon picnic along a stream off Gothic Road. It had been a day that she was certain she would never forget. The young man had been so wonderful, so considerate, so...She closed her eyes and tried to recall the mysterious remark that he had made right before they had said good-bye.

What she remembered most about the mysterious phrasing had something to do with a "big and wonderful" surprise. He had asked if he could meet her for lunch on Monday. He claimed to have something very "special" to tell her. She could not imagine what it was he had in mind, but she was very curious. His ideas, hopes, and desires were becoming very important to her, she realized.

Lunch with him on Monday presented a bit of a problem, though, Kate had explained to him. She had a doctor's appointment scheduled in Gunnison at eleven o'clock. He told her that was not a problem at all. They could go into town together as he needed to pick up a few items anyway. He would shop while she saw the doctor. It seemed like a very good arrangement.

Sitting alone, waiting in Dr. Kellog's outer office was not fun. She kept her mind on the absent young man's mysterious behavior, and tried not to think about what Dr. Kellog would have to say to her. She tried to picture which stores in the town her companion might be browsing while he passed the time waiting for their rendezvous. She had told him she was certain to be finished by twelve, but as she looked at her watch, she could see that the doctor's appointments were running late. She hoped it would not be too much longer.

⌒:∾

Sheriff Stone sat across the small table from Buck Hayden. The interrogation room was so small that Powell stood by the wall and watched the senior officer question the man. For the time being, it appeared that Hayden was more than willing to admit to every charge the Sheriff laid at his doorstep. He agreed to plead guilty on all counts as long as the Sheriff did not try and pin the Clancy murder on him.

He swore, "It's the honest truth. I did not see Big Jim after I left work. I sure as hell didn't kill him. Yeah, I was angry, real angry, but it was more about the money. I was hitching into town and saw that Bronco by the road. I just couldn't resist."

"And Clancy's cabin? You just happened to be driving by?" Stone questioned.

"No, sir. I planned it. After I had those big wheels and all that hauling space, I thought I might as well fill it. It was still dark out, but not long to sun up when I went out there. I didn't want to turn too many lights on or nothin' so as not to draw any lookers. Kind of made a mess looking around, but since the old boy wasn't there, it didn't matter. Nobody at all around to hear nothin'."

"How did you know Clancy wasn't at home when you first got there?" Stone asked.

"Well, sir, that big 4-Runner was nowhere to be seen. Place

134

just had an empty look about it. Can't explain it really, but I didn't take any chances at first. I was real quiet until I looked into the bedroom and saw it was empty."

"What if Clancy had been there? Did you ever think about that? Were you planning to kill him if he were there?"

"No way, Sheriff! More likely he'd kill me. He always had a shotgun handy wherever he went, and he wasn't opposed to using it either. Saw him shoot at that scientist kid once myself."

"Why didn't you come forward about that?" Powell asked.

"Hey, I knew better than to do that. I wasn't about to squeal on my bread and butter," he answered as he turned to look at the standing officer.

"And what about the stolen goods?" the Sheriff probed.

"Got rid of most everything that morning at a flea market in Lake City. Officers got the rest of the stuff when they arrested me," Hayden replied.

"Everything? Are you sure you didn't dump anything in town? Didn't sell anything at all?" Stone continued the questioning.

"Fact is I did sell one item," he hesitated then continued. "Don't want to get anyone else in trouble, though. Kid's plumb innocent."

"Tell us what you sold," the Sheriff insisted.

"A VCR. Had a chance to sell it quick-like to a kid in a parking lot. I thought I needed some ready cash at the time. You know, enough to tide me over to Lake City."

"I think that's all we need from you for now, Hayden. Are you going to press charges against Peek for taking your VW?"

"Naw, long as I get the old van back, I don't really care," the prisoner told them.

Powell spoke up, "That's part of the problem, Mr. Hayden. Peek totalled the van out by Grand Junction."

Hayden looked at the men and then put his head down on his arm for a minute. The lawmen stood watching what would happen next. The man's body began to shake, slightly at first, then he threw back his head and laughed the loudest laugh either of them had ever heard. It was so infectious, that before they knew it they were laughing too. Tears rolled done the captive's cheeks as he howled with laughter and choked out a barely audible sentence.

"I'm not going anywhere anyway!" he forced out the words, and Sheriff Stone nodded in agreement.

Marva Lee Linden was happy to hear from Judge Winfield that his doctor's appointment had gone so well. He told her how he planned to begin a new diet soon, and in the meantime, was planning to do what he called "tapering off" at the table. He explained to her what that meant—he would not take *third* helpings of anything.

He also seemed very pleased to receive the fresh produce from her garden. He enjoyed salads and told her he would be sure and have the vegetables that night. He did not tell her that he was planning to load the leafy lettuce with the creamiest blue cheese dressing in the world. He sensed that the revelation of such indulgence would not go over well with Miss Linden.

⌒⁚∽

It was almost noon when the postmaster himself arrived at Willis Miller's apartment. He knew that such an occasion required him to personally call upon the mail recipient. The envelope within an envelope he carried was certain to shake the small town and make the news. He just hoped that the publicity would not be too harsh for the United States Postal Service.

He stood knocking on Miller's door, waiting for the old veteran to answer. He could hardly wait to see the man's face when he showed him what he had. It was not every day that someone received an undelivered letter postmarked 1946.

24

Deputy Powell was still with Sheriff Stone in Stone's office when the report arrived from Vail.

"Looks like we've found Ms. Mason's motive, Powell. Take a look at this," he said as he handed the junior office the folder.

The young man read the summary sheets and the actual arrest report and follow-up statements. He was surprised and saddened to read that Jim Clancy had been the drunken driver that had crashed into the young Martell couple killing them both. He was even more disturbed to read that Kate Mason was the Martell woman's mother.

"Oh, man. This is rough, Boss. Clancy killed her only child and got nothing more than a fine and a suspended sentence. That would be enough to drive anyone around the bend."

"It's definitely enough to make one consider taking the law into his own hands. I know how I would feel if it happened to my son. Hanging wouldn't be enough!" Stone exclaimed.

"It just doesn't seem fair does it? That daughter was the only family Ms. Mason had," Powell spoke quietly.

"Revenge is evil too. Two wrongs don't make a right sounds pretty weak when you're facing it. But the fact is, you have to consider which is worse: death by automobile accident, or death by a trusted friend who spends months planning the premeditated taking of a life. She must have come here for that purpose. Why, the store, sponsoring the team, and everything must have been just part of her elaborate plan to get back at him. Guess she was savoring the moment."

"Gee, I hate to think that nice lady was plotting like that. Kind of destroys my faith in myself. I was just thinking that I was learning to judge character," he moaned as he spoke.

"Don't be too hard on yourself. Remember we still don't have all of the facts yet. Innocent until proven guilty is still the rule here in this headquarters, Powell," he reminded the younger man.

"It sure does look bad for Ms. Mason, Boss."

"Yes, I know it does. Premeditation would rule out any plea for self defense or accidental shooting. It would go real hard on her in a court."

"Are we going to arrest her?"

"No. Not yet, but we will have to bring her in here for questioning and hear her side of this. She definitely concealed this from us, and I don't appreciate that one bit."

"Maybe she was scared, Boss? If she didn't do it, and she told us she had planned to kill Clancy..." his voice trailed off.

Sheriff Stone told his secretary to place a call to Kate Mason at her shop in Crested Butte. He wanted to talk to the woman immediately.

⚜

Kate was still in with Doctor Kellog when Jeff Harper returned to the doctor's office. He took a seat and waited for Kate to finish. There was no one else in the office since it was lunch time, so he had the place to himself. He switched to another chair that appeared to be more comfortable than the one he first selected. As he settled in to read a magazine, he realized that in the totally quiet office he could hear what the doctor was saying to his patient as the door was not quite closed.

"That's about all of the hope I can offer you. As long as you refuse to do the transfusion, your health will continue to decline. It is only a matter of time. Once winter comes, you will be helpless against the viruses."

"It doesn't really matter, doctor. Hope is a luxury I have not been able to afford for a very long time," the woman replied.

The doctor's door opened, and Kate stepped out and greeted Harper. She made a point of taking the time to introduce the men to each other. Harper was mumbling something to Kellog about being pleased to meet him, but his head was reeling from what he had overheard. He believed he had heard Kate's death sentence. He did not want under any circumstances for her to know that he was

138

aware of the seriousness of her condition.

The doctor bid them farewell and returned to his inner office leaving them alone in the waiting room.

"What is it, Jeff? Are you all right?" she asked noting his pallor.

"Yes. Yes, I'm fine," he spoke rapidly trying frantically to find just the right words for what he was about to say.

"Kate, I have something to tell you," he insisted.

"Can it wait until after lunch? You must be hungry after all that walking around town." she sounded genuinely concerned.

"No. Actually it won't wait. I feel like a fool for having waited this long as it is." He paused and then continued. "The other day when I was late for our tennis game, I told you it was because of a call I had received from D.C."

"I remember, Jeff. I don't see what you are leading to though," she sounded puzzled.

"That call was from my big boss, Dr. Rodman himself. He has offered me that promotion I mentioned to you, and it is effective immediately."

"That's wonderful news!" she exclaimed. "I'm so happy for you. Big pay raise too, I bet."

"There is a pay increase; it goes hand in hand with the cost of living increase that I'll be facing," he spoke hesitantly.

"I don't understand."

"Kate, they have asked me to take over the testing lab we operate on Key West next month."

"Key West! That's the southern tip of Florida. You'll be going there?" she spoke with such sadness in her voice that he wished he had explained the situation differently. It was not turning out the way he had intended.

"It's supposed to be a beautiful place, Kate. There are a lot of flowers and birds."

"I'm sure it is. I know you'll be very happy there," she felt the tears forming in her eyes and her throat seemed to tighten as she spoke.

"No, Kate. I am not going to be happy there," he got her attention with his words. "I'm not going to be happy if I have to go there alone. I want you to come with me."

Kate Mason felt as though her heart would burst with happiness. She knew she loved the man and wanted to be with him. She could not picture life in Crested Butte without her dearest friend.

139

She threw her arms around his neck and he lifted her up to kiss her.

Just as that moment, Sheriff Stone and Deputy Powell walked in the room.

"Excuse me, ma'am," Stone interrupted their happiness. "I phoned your shop and that young girl that works for you told me I might be able to find you here."

"That's quite all right, Sheriff Stone. What can I do for you?" she asked cheerfully, still glowing from the happiness of Harper's proposal.

"I'm afraid I'll have to ask you to accompany us to headquarters."

"Of course, Sheriff," she agreed readily, but inside she could feel her chance for a new life quickly slipping away as she realized that the lawmen must finally know about her true connection to Big Jim Clancy.

~:~

Yvonne Wilson counted her cash. She went through the stack of bills twice and was pleasantly satisfied with the total. She put the large wad of money in an overnight bag that was laid out on her bed next to the other suitcase. Clothing and jewelry were scattered about as the woman selected the few items that would be packed.

It would also be necessary to write a note to Jasper. Yvonne felt certain that he would understand why she needed to go, to get away. He was such a good and generous man, she felt certain that in time he would forgive her for taking their savings and running out on him. The pressure was just becoming more than she could stand. Especially now that the lawmen had the handgun.

She knew the handgun should never have been in the Blazer. It was really foolish for it to be there. If the Sheriff's ballistics' experts decided that the gun was the one used to kill Clancy, she knew that Stone would soon show up on her doorstep to arrest either her or her husband. She did not intend to wait around and find out.

After the bank, she had picked up a one-way airline ticket for herself to Mexico City. There was a direct flight out of Denver if she could get on the Gunnison connection later that afternoon. Checking the time, she knew that she had only an hour or so to wait until she needed to go to the airport. For her, it was not much time to make such an important wardrobe decision.

⁓

Willis Miller sat at the kitchen table reading and rereading the letter he had just received from the postmaster. He could not believe his eyes, but it was as plain as could be. The letter had remained undelivered for more than forty years. It did not seem possible to him, but there it was.

He read again the faded ink of the letter and tears came to his eyes. The news was so good and so wonderful that he knew he had to take action at once. He just was not sure what action to take. Then he thought of Miss Linden and Judge Winfield and realized that they might be able to help him. Goosebumps shivered on his skin as he looked again at the postmark and return address in West Virginia. More than two years after the war and a long time after Miller had returned from Europe, as impossible as it seemed, there it was. The signature at the bottom of the letter was none other than that of his friend and comrade, Ed Campbell!

25

Sheriff Stone asked Jeff Harper to wait outside his office while he and Powell questioned Kate Mason. The young man reluctantly agreed, but told the lady that he would be happy to call an attorney for her if she wished. She thanked him and assured him that it would not be necessary.

Seated in the Sheriff's Office, Kate did not feel quite as confident as the words she had spoken would have led Harper to believe. She sat quietly waiting for the lawmen to ask the questions that she had been waiting for so long to answer. The fact that both men seemed to be shuffling papers and folders rather than interrogating her was confusing. The silence was starting to bother her.

"Sheriff," she finally had to break the tension. "You said you had some important matters to discuss. I really wish we could get this over with. I was planning to go to lunch with Dr. Harper." She sounded impatient.

"Just a minute, ma'am," Stone told her firmly. "I want all of these papers to be in order before we take your statement."

Powell recognized that Stone was deliberately stalling trying to raise the tension and anxiety level of the woman. Stone was going for the whole truth from her this time, and he was doing it on his own territory, in his own way. Powell just observed the lady.

She was getting more nervous wondering why Stone did not come right out and accuse her of the Clancy murder. At least then she would have a chance to state her case; but until he accused her, she was not about to divulge anything.

"Well, I guess we're ready to proceed," Stone told them cheerfully. "I believe we got all of the particulars, full name, address, etc. the last time we spoke."

"Really Sheriff, we're not going to rehash what we talked about last time, are we?"

"Oh, no, ma'am! There have been some interesting new developments in the case. I'm sure you'll be happy to know that we were able to find your gun." He let the information sink in while he watched her reaction.

"Your gun has gone in to Ballistics, and there should be a report on it momentarily."

Kate Mason sat looking at him but did not move a muscle. She was obviously in complete control, Powell observed.

"Ma'am, there are one or two other things that we would also like to clear up right now."

"Here it comes!" she thought and tried not to give away the fear she was feeling.

"We have confirmed your story that you were at the crime scene at approximately the time Clancy was shot. There is physical evidence as well as two witnesses."

"Two? I only spoke to one old man. The one I told you about."

"Someone else saw you there," the Sheriff told her. He was hoping he could get her to admit that she had seen Yvonne Wilson there as well since Willis Miller told him that they had both been there at the same time. He needed to know the truth because so far there was no confirmation of the fact that Mrs. Wilson had been anywhere near the scene.

"Someone else? You must mean the woman. I did pass a woman on the footpath through the tall weeds. I didn't know who she was though."

"Can you describe her?" Stone needed answers.

"Not really. She just sort of hurried past me. Dark hair, I think. Bright makeup. Nice clothes."

"Yvonne Wilson," Powell told her.

Sheriff Stone wanted more answers but needed to change direction for the moment. He wanted to find out about her motive.

"Ma'am, it has come to our attention that before you moved here you lived in Vail. Is that correct?"

"Yes, it is."

"Is it also true that your daughter was killed in a traffic accident there last year?"

"Yes, Sheriff. I see you have the facts."

"Ma'am, I have reason to believe that you moved here from

143

Vail with the express purpose of killing Mr. Clancy in order to avenge your daughter's death. You can stop me if I'm wrong."

"You are not wrong, Sheriff Stone. I admit that it was my intent to kill Jim Clancy. I bought the gun for that purpose, and I carried it in my purse waiting for a chance to kill him." She spoke so calmly that neither Powell nor Stone could understand it at the time.

"But, I assure you both, I did not kill Big Jim. I merely went there that day to see him and cancel out the date. I decided I wanted to spend the evening with Jeff...err Dr. Harper. Pure and simple. I panicked when I saw that he had been shot. I was terrified that I would be blamed. For a brief moment, I even wondered if maybe I had lost my mind and actually done it. I had planned it for so long."

"Why should we believe your story? You had the means, the motive, and a weapon to do the job."

"Won't the ballistics people be able to clear my gun after they test it?"

"Only if you are innocent."

"Well, I am I tell you. Someone else had to have done it. Maybe it was that old guy or that woman with the nice clothes and the weird boots." She sounded very upset.

Instantly, both Sheriff Stone and Deputy Powell were alert. They listened intently to her answer as Stone asked, "What do you mean by 'weird boots?' Did they look strange or what?"

Kate told them, "Maybe 'weird' wasn't exactly the right word. I just noticed that she was nicely dressed, but had on a pair of old, muddy boots. She walked like they were too large for her. Really they were just boots like you would keep in your car or on your back porch. You know, a pair of grubbies to put on when you don't want to ruin your good shoes. It was so muddy out there, it took me a long time to clean my own shoes when I got home."

The lawmen did not hear her last sentence as they were already on their feet and heading toward the door with the search warrant the Sheriff had pulled from the desk drawer. But, before they could leave the surprised woman, the telephone rang loudly.

Stone turned and hurriedly grabbed the phone; it was Ballistics!

꒳⋮꒳

The Sheriff's jeep and two squad cars arrived with sirens and flashing lights at the Jasper Wilson residence. Blocking the drive-

144

way, they could see the fright in the eyes of Yvonne Wilson as she set her suitcases down beside the old car.

She offered no resistance as the female officer handcuffed her and took her to the squad car. She did ask Sheriff Stone to notify her husband, and he assured her that he would.

By Labor Day, things had changed in Gunnison County, Colorado. Although it had only been slightly more than a month since the arrest of Yvonne Wilson for the murder of Big Jim Clancy, life was returning to normal for those persons most directly involved in the case.

Jasper Wilson remained ever faithful by his wife's side during the hearings and the Grand Jury indictment. He was able to hire a good lawyer who felt certain that Mrs. Wilson would not be found guilty of first degree murder, but rather would face the consequences of a charge of death-by-accidental-shooting.

Mrs. Wilson had freely confessed to shooting Clancy, but claimed she did not intend to kill him. Her statement was that she thought the gun was unloaded. She told no one that the reason the gun was in the Blazer in the first place was so that she could accompany her husband to the construction site and bury the weapon under the concrete pourings. She had simply neglected to get up early enough to go to the site with him.

Her motive for shooting Clancy remained a mystery. She told the investigators that she had only met with Clancy to pick up the money that he had told her he would loan her. She said it was obvious when she arrived at the Roaring Judy that Clancy did not have any money with him. Because they were such good friends for so long, she was only joking when she took the gun out of her oversized purse to pretend to rob him. Clancy reached for the gun, and it had gone off accidentally, she repeated each time she was asked to give a statement.

Yvonne never said anything about the way Clancy had used her and dumped her. That would remain her secret. She believed that she would die of humiliation if anyone knew the truth, after all, she had a certain status to maintain in the county.

With the help of Miss Linden and Judge Winfield, Willis Miller was able to trace the current whereabouts of his friend, Ed Campbell. He shaved, showered and dressed in new clothes before he left Gunnison to meet up with his old pal in West Virginia. He looked like a new man, a prosperous one at that. (Miss Linden was overheard to remark to Winfield that Miller might finally shut-up now that he knew his friend had also survived the war.) In any event, the old veteran had a lot of catching up to do with his comrade.

Sheriff Stone had been particularly pleased to receive a postcard from Kate and Jeff Harper in Key West. They wrote that they had just arrived and found the place to be as beautiful as they had imagined. With the proceeds from the sales of Kate's shop in Crested Butte, she was considering buying another small business, probably something to do with dolphins. Both were well and enjoying the warm, tropical sun.

Outside of the office, Stone had not seen much of Tim Powell in the past two or three weeks. Now that the Clancy Case was closed, the young lawman seemed to be spending a great deal of time with a certain Linda Lou. When he was not with her, he was talking about her *ad nauseum* as far as Stone was concerned, but he did not want to discourage the boy. Powell's happiness was important to him. He had the makings of a fine lawman, Stone affirmed.

As for the Sheriff of Gunnison County, Frank B. Stone, he was having the time of his life during the Labor Day holiday. It was the final softball game of the season. As the last man up to bat in the last inning of a tied 0-0 game and one man on base, Stone felt the pressure of the play. He could hear his own son's voice in the crowd cheering him on as he stepped to the plate.

Taking careful aim with a watchful eye, Stone readied himself for the pitch. In seconds, his powerful bat met the ball sending it out of the ballpark for a homerun!

The Hummers finished the season with a win: 2-0.

THE END

About the Author

J.C. Franklin is an award-winning author currently residing in New Mexico. She is a member of the Southwest Writers Workshop in Albuquerque. J.C. is originally from the State of Maine and has travelled extensively. She spends a part of every year in the area around Gunnison County, Colorado. Her novel, *Gunnison*, is the first in a series about a fictional County Sheriff, Frank Stone.